Jen

THE BRIGHTONIANS

My love letter to our wonderful city-by-the-sea

By
Daren Kay

x
Daren

GHP
Grosvenor House
Publishing Limited

The right of Daren Kay to be identified as the author of this
work has been asserted in accordance with Section 78
of the Copyright, Designs and Patents Act 1988

The book cover is copyright to Daren Kay

This book is published by
Grosvenor House Publishing Ltd
Link House
140 The Broadway, Tolworth, Surrey, KT6 7HT.
www.grosvenorhousepublishing.co.uk

This book is a work of fiction. Any resemblance to
people or events, past or present, is purely coincidental.

A CIP record for this book
is available from the British Library

ISBN 978-1-83975-437-1

For Gary & Rory, and all the Brightonians
who inspired and encouraged me along the way…

BRIG

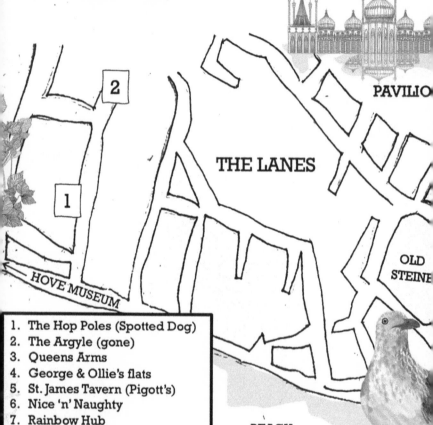

PAVILIO

PAVILIO

THE LANES

OLD
STEINE

HOVE MUSEUM

BEACH

1. The Hop Poles (Spotted Dog)
2. The Argyle (gone)
3. Queens Arms
4. George & Ollie's flats
5. St. James Tavern (Pigott's)
6. Nice 'n' Naughty
7. Rainbow Hub
8. Adam's flat
9. Miss Blythe's flat
10. Cameron & Alex's house
* Some notable LGBTQ+ venues

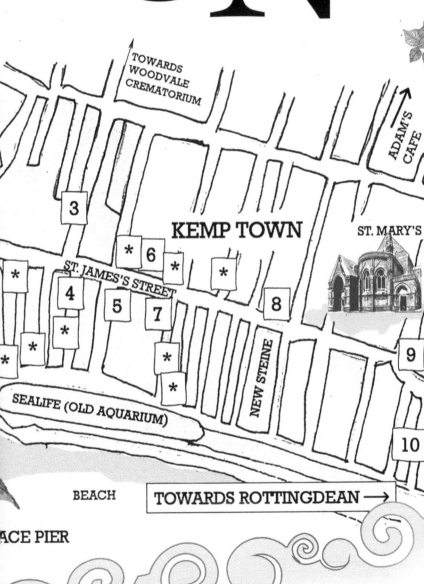

TON

TOWARDS
WOODVALE
CREMATORIUM

ADAM'S
CAFE

3

KEMP TOWN

ST. MARY'S

* 6

*

*

*

ST. JAMES'S STREET

4

5 7

8

*

*

*

*

9

NEW STEINE

*

SEALIFE (OLD AQUARIUM)

10

BEACH

TOWARDS ROTTINGDEAN →

ACE PIER

FOREWORD

Brighton is a special place. Like so many gay enclaves around the world, such as NYC's Greenwich Village, Berlin's Schöneberg or Green Point in Cape Town, it is a scene of sanctuary, inclusivity, freedom to be yourself, and fun.

Of course, Brighton does have its own 'gay village': The St James's Street area of Kemp Town (where much of this book is set). But in reality, the whole city is such - a wonderful, higgledy-piggledy mishmash of buildings encompassed by hills to the north and sea to the south that seem to form a 360-degree big gay hug. (Our exotic, Grade I Royal Pavilion sits at the heart of the action, and even its India-inspired domes and minarets are floodlit in pink for camp city occasions.)

I recall, while strolling the seafront in my early twenties, being branded a 'faggot' by a shouty man-in-a-van resembling a human/bulldog hybrid and, after a short breather, *smiling*, safe in the belief that here, in contrast to so many other places, the city was on my side.

This idea is amplified to tangible levels during our Pride festival when, seemingly, the entire city is painted in rainbow colours to celebrate diversity, togetherness, and the brilliant LGBTQ+ residents past and present who shape this sparkly seaside city. *The Brightonians* captures the essence of all this.

As the novel flits between Brighton in 1965 and 2019, the characters draw attention to the challenges faced by the

LGBTQ+ community over the last fifty-or-so years. It delves into the notion that queerness is not just about sex or sexuality, but about the humour and compassion that is at the heart of our community. The queer characters in the novel aren't victims, hiding in ghettos, but comfortable in their own skins and at one with the world around them. The city that holds them.

Not since E.F. Benson's *Mapp & Lucia* have I so speedily fallen in love with such an array of fabulous characters. And not since Armistead Maupin's *Tales of the City,* have I read a novel that so perceptively describes the queer city in which it is set. If you, too, count yourself as a Brightonian, I hope you will see something of yourself in the friends you are about to make within these pages. And if you have yet to discover this city's quirky charms, I hope that after enjoying *The Brightonians* you will count yourself as an honorary one.

Torsten Højer, Brighton, 2021.
Editor of the queer anthology *Speak My Language and Other Stories* (Robinson, 2015)

PREFACE

After almost 30 years writing copy to sell everything from margarine to motor cars, in 2016 I took a leap of faith, quit my job at one of the UK's biggest ad agencies, and began writing about the things that really made me open my laptop with glee every day. The result is in your hands. A novel about all the stuff I love. Brighton, of course. Its cheeky, happy-go-lucky ambience that seems to shout *'do what you want'* from every street corner.

And more importantly, the irreverent, smart, talented and funny people that have made the city their home. Especially those who live in Kemp Town, the beating heart of the LGBTQ+ community.

Returning to live here in 2015 – after 25 years in London – I was thrilled that the city and its residents had lost none of their unique charm and I knew immediately that it was something I wanted to capture in my writing.

For the plot itself, I wanted to draw on my other great passion: history. So, it seemed serendipitous that during the first draft of *The Brightonians*, I became involved in two projects that greatly influenced the plot of my novel.

First, a mould-breaking exhibition at Brighton Museum that aimed to celebrate the city's queer heritage – called *Queer the Pier*. And secondly, a mobile phone-based walking tour of Brighton's queer past, created by community publishing group, Queen Spark Books.

It was through my involvement with both these projects that I became aware how much queer history has been actively erased, carefully hidden or simply lost. And with the ephemera that has survived mostly locked away in archives or private collections, it also struck me how important it was to find more accessible ways to bring these histories to life to new generations of queer people and their allies.

Hopefully, the flashbacks in my novel to 1960s Brighton do just that. And if they trigger an interest in finding out more about the extraordinary lives of ordinary queer people before the days of Pride and Trans Pride, then so much better. It is something that I plan to follow up in subsequent stories in the series.

But in the meantime, I hope you enjoy getting to know Bette, Ollie, Izzy and Cameron – as much as I enjoyed creating them. So, pour yourself a G&T and find a comfortable chair. The show is about to begin…

Daren Kay

ACKNOWLEDGEMENTS

To Nathan and Justin, from Inkandescent Publishing, for their invaluable advice on the wordy and unwieldy first draft. Corinna Edwards-Colledge for her encouragement to just 'go for it'. David Harkins, for advising on Scottish dialogue. Alexia Lazou, Grace Brindle and Kevin Bacon from Brighton & Hove Museum. Alexia for fact-checking the accuracy of the chapters on Brighton's cinematic heritage*. Grace and Kevin for allowing me to mention Hove Museum by name.

Alf le Flohic for casting his gimlet eye over the text and his in-depth knowledge of Brighton's queer past. All the collectors and volunteers I met during the curation of *Queer the Pier*. Ali Ghanimi and John Riches from Queen Spark Books, for introducing me to *Daring Hearts* – the definitive guide to queer life in Brighton in the 50s and 60s, published in collaboration with Brighton Ourstory. Sarah Arnett for her beautiful design for the front cover.

Sarah Reese from Global Butterflies for her advice on portraying Grace Davidson. Fr. Andrew, vicar at St. Mary's, Kemp Town and Bishop's Liaison Officer LGBT+ for allowing me to set several chapters in St. Mary's. Kate, Phil, Simon, Trish and Emma from Nice 'n' Naughty for agreeing to let me mention the famous window of their Brighton branch. John Fletcher for letting me name-check the Queens Arms, Kemp Town, and for Miss Jason and Davina Sparkle for being my 'dancing queens' at Grace's wake. Ian Berry for allowing me to allude to his art-work being used for the campaign to relaunch fictional gin brand, Rakewell's. Tilly Hunt for her enthusiasm and expertise in social media. Nikki Gatenby for helping me craft my marketing strategy. Hugh Ross for voicing my trailer and Dan Turvil for filming it. Torsten Højer for writing my Foreword and co-ordinating my PR. Grosvenor House Publishing for giving me (and hundreds of aspiring writers) the chance to shine.

My wonderful book reviewers – the Brightonians who appear in the next two pages. And Luke, Brian, Mum, Dad and my sister, Helen, who – though not residents of our wonderful city-by-the-sea – are very much Brightonians at heart.

And finally, the thousands of seagulls who have watched my every move over the last three years… and still do!

* Researched from various online sources including Collection Search – BFI - British Film Institute, Brightonfilm.com and IMDb.

REVIEWS FROM SOME 'REAL' BRIGHTONIANS

"A very witty insight into the kaleidoscope that is Brighton life…" David Harkins, artist.

"A rollicking and witty tale, that shows Brighton beyond the picture-postcards and candy-floss." Corinna Edwards-Colledge, author.

"Brimming with characters you can't help but adore… despite their flaws." Gary Moyle, Charity Fundraiser.

"Daren has put into words the colour that makes Brighton so inspiring to me in my work." Sarah Arnett, artist and designer.

"Armed with cocktail sticks and razor-sharp tongues, the Brighton set described by Daren take competitive partying and social one-upmanship to new and ever more hilarious levels." Rory Smith, artist and advertising strategist.

"Touching, funny, thrilling… *The Brightonians* has mini-series written all over it!" Dan Turvil, film maker.

"What a gorgeous warm treat. I felt so at home whilst being invited into a familiar world with a new twist." Kim Hunt, entrepreneur and fashion journalist.

"The characters are so life-like, you can hear them as you read. Like eavesdropping on a conversation in the pub." Matthew Lee, entrepreneur and club owner/DJ.

"Drinking, swearing and historical flash-backs – consider my fancy well and truly tickled." Alf le Flohic, writer and historian.

"Diversity, togetherness, and the brilliant LGBTQ+ residents past and present who shape this sparkly seaside city. *The Brightonians* captures the essence of all this." Torsten Højer, writer and journalist.

"I defy anyone not to fall in love with the cantankerous old hound, Mr Ben." Sarah Clarke, dog owner and advertising executive.

"From the bay window of my flat in St. James's Street, I see colourful characters like the ones in *The Brightonians* every day of the week. And now, thanks to Daren's eye for comic detail, so will you." Stuart Barrett, Ballroom & Latin dancer.

"As a copywriter, Daren was amongst the best in the business. As a storyteller, his first novel does not disappoint." Nikki Gatenby, entrepreneur, author and PR expert.

"This is a great read. Captures the sauce, seediness and plain good fun of gay Brighton life. With a bit of mystery thrown in. Terrific." Hugh Ross, actor.

PROLOGUE

I've been keeping watch over this city for centuries.

Long before the doughnut-topped observation tower looked down on the rusty carcass of the West Pier. Years before Constable painted the fishing boats that once littered its rugged coastline. And even before Doctor Russell recommended its seawater as a universal panacea.

Gliding over its pebbly beaches and looking down from its rooftops, over the years, I've seen it all.

A modest farmhouse turned into a fantasy palace for a fun-loving prince. Rows of terraces thrown up to accommodate his entourage of hangers-on. And, with the arrival of the railway, its gradual shift from pleasure-garden of the privileged to candy-floss-scented playground of the masses. No longer a place where the upper-classes would come to be seen for the Season, but one where furtive couples come to be anonymous for a 'dirty weekend'. And more recently still, I've seen it become the destination for parties of women with nothing more in common than a bride-to-be and the urge to wander through the city's narrow lanes clutching inflatable penises.

Yet despite all these changes, one thing has remained constant; the reason people come here. Oh yes, it might be B R I G H T O N that runs through the sticks of rock sold on every street corner. But the word that runs through the city itself is as true today as it was in Doctor Russell's day.

F R E E D O M.

Freedom to kiss someone quick – and squeeze them slowly. Freedom to do things you wouldn't dare do at home. Freedom to be whoever you want to be.

And nowhere is this freedom more visible than along St. James's Street; the thoroughfare of pubs, cafés, sex shops and tattoo parlours that is the main artery into the city's gay quarter. It's also the place from where today – perched high on the roof of St. Mary's church – I have a bird's eye view of the city.

But the weekend is over. The tourists have gone home and the only creatures I can see paddling in the sea this cold October morning are the gigantic three-armed beasts on the horizon; their vast sails harnessing the force of nature that once powered the windmills Mr Constable was so fond of capturing on canvas.

Even so, there is plenty to observe still. There are, of course, the fascinating people who have made this far-from-quintessential seaside town their home; the people who proudly refer to themselves as *Brightonians*.

And in particular, the lucky folk who are about to receive one of the handwritten black and gold envelopes I see a postman taking from his satchel in the street below.

First of all, there is the couple that lives in the mauve townhouse in Wyndham Street. Assuming the envelope contains an invitation to something or other, the recipient here will resist the temptation to open it alone. After a short deliberation, he will instead place it on the dining-room table in wait for his husband's return from work. Next to see their name in golden calligraphic curls will be the custodian of the building on which I am now perched. He'll have to be quick though; otherwise it will have to be wrestled from the jaws of a sharp-toothed hound called Mr Ben before the contents can be appreciated. And then there is the occupant of the flat that looks onto the square of grass known to locals as the New Steine. Since he did not return home last night, his envelope will wait in purgatory at the bottom of a metal post-box in the communal hall. And finally, there is the denizen who lives on the corner of lower St. James's Street. Still wrapped in the arms of Morpheus – or whichever future Mr Right occupies his dreams at this moment in time – his will be placed at the foot of his stairs by a neighbour who is likely to be wearing a little bit more make-up than you'd expect for a seventy-three-year-old man.

But since this neighbourhood is home to some of the city's most colourful residents, no one will bat an eyelid – eye-shadowed or otherwise.

Indeed, it is a quirk with which you shall soon be familiar – because in order for our story to begin – it is to this particular *Brightonian* that we must now fly…

Chapter One

Just you and me now, kiddo!

Monday 7th October 2019 – 8am – St. James's Street, Kemp Town

Rudely awoken by the ringing at the other end of the flat, George Gibbons prised himself out of bed and drowsily felt for his slippers on the floor. A little stiff from the October chill, he felt his old bones groan as he did so. *Who could possibly be calling me at this hour?* he thought to himself as he pulled on his dressing gown and shuffled down the corridor to the impatient telephone.

'Hello?' he said, pressing his good ear to the receiver and staring suspiciously into the mouthpiece.

'Sorry to call so early,' said the voice at the other end. 'But you said to let you know as soon as it happened.'

What a silly sausage he was. It was the care home, of course. *Who else would it be at this time in the morning?*

'She's gone. About half an hour ago.'

'Oh, Gracie…' replied the old man, hearing his voice disappearing into thin air. 'Well, she said it would be today,' he added cheerily after a few seconds. 'On time, as always!'

It was now the turn of the caller to be lost for words. Sensing from the silence at the other end of the phone that his comment was not quite in keeping with the tone of the situation, George thanked them for letting him know and agreed to be in touch. But just as he thought they were about to say goodbye…

'Oh, sorry, I almost forgot!'

'Yes, dear?'

'About the funeral. Before Grace went, she mentioned something about… *a wish-list*. She said you'd understand what she meant.'

George reassured the person at the other end of the phone that he did – and politely ended the call. As he returned the receiver to its resting place, he caught the reflection of two faces in the hall mirror. His own – somewhat saggy and lined, remnants of last night's face cream still clinging to the crevices around his eyes. And a much younger one – a boy of about 18 or 19, with blond hair and cherubic lips; his blue eyes beaming at George from the framed cover of a magazine on the wall behind him.

'Just you and me now, kiddo!' said George, turning to face the teenager and sinking into the chair next to the telephone. Allowing his eyes to linger on the picture for a while, he felt a smile curl across his face. The boy in the frame smiled back at him, exactly as he had done for as long as George could remember. But no sooner had the words left his lips than a new thought entered his head. *Now, what did I do with Grace's wish-list?*

Easing himself up from the chair, he walked the few feet into the kitchen towards a built-in cupboard in the corner of the room. 'Ah, there you are,' he whispered to himself, retrieving a small blue tin from deep inside. Rusty and caked in dust, he took it over to the kitchen sink, gave it a wipe with a damp cloth and then made his way to the table in the bay window.

Ordinarily the ideal spot to spy upon the comings and goings of St. James's Street, at this early hour there was nothing much to see – except the postman in the street below and a seagull perched on the window-ledge opposite. For some reason, George felt he was being observed by the old bird. But with far more pressing matters to attend to, he dismissed the thought and made himself comfortable at the table. Picking up the butter knife he'd grabbed from the drainer, he slid the blade under the lid of the tin and for the first time in years, came face to face with the neatly arranged treasures inside. A bundle of letters tied up with red ribbon; a few rusty old badges with slogans like 'Stop the Clause' and 'ACT UP'; a fragment of glass wrapped in tissue paper; and on top of them all, a pair of wool booties. Removing the bundle, he pushed the tin and its remaining contents to the back of the table. Ribbon untied, he quickly found what he was looking for: *The last wishes of Grace Davidson.* Remembering the evening he and Grace had drunkenly drawn up a list of requests for their respective funerals, he shook his head and tutted. *Clearly, he would now need to give his list to someone else!*

After taking a deep breath, George glanced over the words his friend had written all those years ago. *Oh, Gracie!* he sighed, before placing it to one side. He was about to retie the bundle of old letters when quite unexpectedly his eyes fell upon a folded sheet of paper bearing a word in the same hand as the note that he'd just read. Underlined in capitals, it simply said: RAGAZZI. George froze for a moment. *My goodness, what on earth is that doing in here!* Regaining his composure, he carefully unfolded the note and spread it out on the table. As he did so, the yellowing paper released an odour that was oddly familiar to him. Sweet and musty, like walking into an old barn on a warm day. Ding, ding, ding, chimed his grey cells suddenly. He knew it was just his memory playing tricks on him, but he couldn't help being transported back to 'that' summer all those years ago. Spurred on by these memories, his heart pounding in his chest, he quickly scanned over the letter in silence until something about the last few sentences compelled him to read them out aloud.

'Hopefully, our paths will cross again in the future. In this life. Or the next,' said George to an empty kitchen. 'Well, you're all together now, dear,' he chuckled to himself. *But was he by himself?* Just then, for the second time that morning, he found he was being observed. The seagull from before had flown over to his side of the street and was now staring at him from the ledge of his bay window.

'Buzz off! Feathers!' snapped George, tapping the pane with one of his red-polished fingernails.

Head cocked to one side, the seagull locked eyes with him for a moment, squawked its familiar haha-haha cackle and launched itself into the air.

'Damned bird,' muttered George under his breath, reaching for Grace's *wish-list* and putting it in his dressing-gown pocket. As he did so, he caught his reflection in the bay window.

'OK,' he said to the ghostly image. 'Let's go and make Grace's wishes come true!'

Chapter Two

Cameron's train of thought

Born and bred in Perthshire, Cameron MacIntyre had been happily immersed in an article about a new Scottish-Jamaican restaurant that had just opened in Tooting when he was alerted to the voice crackling through the tannoy.

'... Grace Davidson has died.'

Wrenched away from the delights of yam haggis fritters by the mention of a familiar name, he tuned in to the rest of the announcement.

'On behalf of my colleagues, I would like to offer my sincerest condolences on this sad occasion...'

Momentarily interrupted by a sob, the voice pulled itself together and continued.

'Thank you for your attention. We wish you a pleasant onward journey.'

A message for the passengers on the train? Or was it perhaps meant for Grace Davidson's recently departed soul? It was all Cameron could do not to snigger. Not that anyone would have clocked. The frenzy of activity created by the announcement was almost immediate. Who was Grace Davidson? What did she look like? Why had they announced it on the train? Just a few of the questions he could hear being whispered, or, he suspected, being typed into internet search engines on phones and laptops all around him. Of course, not everyone on the train was in the mirk about Grace Davidson. Anyone like himself, taking the train all the way to Brighton that evening, would know exactly who she was. In fact, even to a relatively new Brightonian like Cameron, Grace was a household name.

'God bless her,' sighed a wee lassie at his table, staring wistfully at the ceiling.

'It's the end of an era,' he heard a man in front say to a fellow passenger.

And from someone behind him, he was sure he also heard the slightly inappropriate, 'Do you think we'll get the day off?'

He looked at the time on his phone. 17.47pm. *That's where I was when I heard that Grace Davidson had popped her clogs. On a train surrounded by a bunch of strangers.* And then it struck him. No messages! Was he the first in his circle to hear the news? There was no time to spare. Moments later, Cameron had found a photo of Grace, pilfered some words from an article about Harvey Milk – the gay politician to whom she was often compared – and typed a heartfelt obituary into his Instagram feed.

'More than a mayor and an MP, Grace Davidson was a visionary. She imagined a better world and set about creating it. RIP Gracie. Long live the vision you made real.' #gracedavidson #Gracie #brightonMP #brightonmayor #RIPmayor #RIPMP

Less than five minutes after the announcement on the train's tannoy system – with the sleight of hand a magician would envy – Cameron had become the bearer of bad news for thousands of his friends and followers on social media.

Yet as he put down his phone, there was one friend in particular he had in his mind's eye; Isobel Pitt, a recent addition to his social circle with whom he had enjoyed several jousting matches of late. Armed with cocktail sticks rather than lances, the competition was no less feisty, and it was clear that this formidable socialite – fresh off the boat from London – was on a mission to usurp Cameron's hard-fought position at the centre of things in his adopted hometown. Being the first to deliver news of Grace Davidson's death was a significant coup in Cameron's campaign to keep Isobel at bay. *Put that in your wee pipe and smoke it, missie!* he thought to himself as he pressed send.

The unexpected distractions made the time fly quicker than usual. No sooner had he put down his phone than the train pulled into Gatwick, deposited three quarters of its passengers and triggered a collective sigh of relief from those left onboard. Enjoying the extra space, Cameron returned his attention to the unread pages of his newspaper, which largely meant scanning the sports section for photos of cute men in shorts. Owing to patchy phone reception from Gatwick onwards, after he'd done that there was little to do but flick through the day's phone messages; the most interesting of which was a WhatsApp he'd got that morning from his husband. In the photo, Alex – his other half – was holding a black and gold envelope and pursing his lips in an 'ooh err missus' pose. From the pout and accompanying message – *We shall go to the ball!* – Cameron deduced it was an invite to something. He zoomed in to see if he recognised the handwriting crafted in beautiful – but anonymous – calligraphic script. He did not. What he did recognise, however, was the boy he'd fallen in love with two decades earlier. There were more laughter lines around his puppy dog eyes – and his nose hair could do with a bit of a pluck – but at 42, Alex still bore a passing resemblance to the handsome singer in a boyband that Cameron used to like. Warmed by this fact, he scrolled down to the other hot news just in from his husband; they were out of milk. As he made a mental note to pick some up at the station, his phone suddenly sprang into action. It was a call from work. But just as he was about to answer, the train plunged into a tunnel. *Thank fuck for that!* thought Cameron. Yet the real joy of reaching the Downs was the sense of freedom that awaited him on the other side. Not only did the sky appear higher, giving him the sensation of a weight being lifted off his shoulders, but from this point onwards, the wheels on the track seemed to be sweetly singing 'nearly home, nearly home'.

To pass the few minutes below ground, Cameron busied himself with the other great love of his life: himself. Turning to the train window, temporarily transformed into a mirror by the darkness of the tunnel, he pawed at his ginger beard and ran his fingers through his thick mane of red hair cut just above the collar of his smart designer suit; one of several he wore for his job as group account director at London's hippest advertising agency – Zarathustra. And while the years had been less kind to his pale Scottish skin than they had to Alex's age-defying hide, the dermatologist's injections had more than made up for what Father Time had inflicted upon him. A prick of Botox here, a smidgeon of filler there. When it came to advertising, no one could accuse Cameron of not practising what he preached. MOT complete, he stared admiringly at the face staring back at him in the glass until – whoosh. As if by magic, the mirror – and his reflection – disappeared.

Thankfully for Cameron, leaving the tunnel brought with it new delights: the rewards of his social media bombshell. Signal restored, he noted the numbers merrily totting up in the little red circles next to the various apps on his phone. Accordingly, he allowed himself that mischievous little smile he had earlier been denied. A wonderfully satisfying moment, which was shattered only seconds later by the announcement of an incoming call.

'Oliver Simpson. Oliver Simpson,' sang the automated voice on his phone.

'Here we go,' said Cameron. 'No rest for the wicked!'

Chapter Three

For the Grace of God!

Monday 7th October 2019 – 18.30pm –
St. James's Street, Kemp Town

'Oh Em Gee!' squealed Ollie down the phone.

'Aye, Grace Davidson. I know. They announced it on the train,' replied Cameron to his friend.

'No. I mean. Oh Em Gee! *St. James's Street.*'

'*St. James's Street.* Why? What's happened?'

'Hang on a minute. I'll send you a piccy,' replied Ollie, striding over to the window.

'One moment, caller,' he sang down the phone, before opening the camera and zooming into the shop window of Nice 'n' Naughty on the other side of the street. Known throughout Brighton for their arresting window displays, Ollie's focus today was not, however, their impressive selection of latex underwear, harnesses and rubber fetish gear. Instead, he picked out the two showroom dummies wrapped from head to toe in black bedsheets. Photo taken, Ollie sent it to Cameron and returned to his sofa.

'Look! Even Charles and Diana are in mourning!' he trilled into his phone.

'Jesus Christ. Noooo. That's priceless!' replied Cameron.

'I know! But I bet Diana's still wearing the sexy maid's outfit she's had on all week.'

'Aye. Though it does look like someone's at least taken the dildo out of Charles' jockstrap. And is that a framed photo of Grace I can see on that wee pedestal?'

'Sure is. It's one of the leaflets about the candlelit vigil they're organising tonight in front of the AIDS statue-thingy. That cute Korean boy from the Rainbow Hub handed me one just now.'

'Oh wow. What time's it start?'

'Eight o'clock, it says.'

'Great. I can change first. Anyone good gonna be speaking?'

'Dunno, it's all a bit last minute. There's a link on the flyer though. I'll have a look in a mo. Perhaps Bette will be doing something. I'm pretty sure she and Grace were quite pally. I'll pop up and ask her.'

'Good plan! She might even have some intel on the funeral. See what else you can find out.'

'OK,' replied Ollie, sensing his friend was hatching something. But before he could ask what Cameron had in mind…

'Shite. Train's pulling in. Gotta—'

Conversation over, Ollie's thoughts turned to his fact-finding mission upstairs. He sniffed his sweatshirt. *Shower first, I think.* Still wearing the clothes that he wore for his job as a personal trainer, Ollie made his way to the bathroom to freshen up. Standing in front of the mirror a few minutes later, now naked except for the towel wrapped around his waist, he gave his body a once over. The water from the shower had turned his chest hair into a forest of black spirals. But in amongst them, he was shocked to see one or two grey hairs lurking there too. He'd already taken to shaving his head to hide his premature baldness. *How long would it be before he had to take the clippers to his chest as well*? Coupled with thoughts of the upcoming vigil, the sight of his semi-naked body got Ollie thinking about his *own* mortality. Thirty-five next birthday! Where had the time gone? He pinched his cheeks and stroked his chin. *He could still pass for 30, though, couldn't he? In the right light.* It was true. Despite the five o'clock shadow, his skin still had a youthful glow about it. He had his Caribbean dad to thank for that. And from his Brummie mummy, he had inherited a cute button nose and chubby cheeks – which people often said gave him a baby face. The very slight hint of a tummy peeping out from the top of his towel was, however, one feature he couldn't pin on his folks. That was down entirely to the pubs and clubs of Kemp Town. He stroked his midriff and breathed in. A few more circuit training sessions and a few less nights on the town should see him right, he reassured himself. *And 35 wasn't so old, was it?* Still time to snare a husband before he slipped into the *'hello, sexy daddy'* bracket. But how? Not through any of the dating sites he was on. What had Cameron said once? The odds are good, but the goods are odd. He wasn't wrong. Certainly, the chances of finding someone to be his 'plus one' in time for the party he'd received an invite to that morning didn't seem very high. Especially as it was fancy-dress! *Who did he have to go as again?* Thankfully, the sound of his neighbour's footsteps on the floor above saved him from having to think about that particular dilemma for now.

'Oh fuck! The vigil!' he said out loud, remembering his promise to Cameron. But on opening his wardrobe, he found himself presented with an even more pressing costume-related question. *What do you wear to a candlelit vigil?* Was black too formal? Perhaps something a bit more celebratory. A rainbow flag over my shoulders maybe? That could work.

As long as it's not flammable. *Was it flammable?* To be fair, being a tracky-bottom-wearing fitness instructor, fashion wasn't Ollie's strong suit. And candlelit-vigil-wear wasn't something he'd ever had to consider before. Just as he was in danger of being side-tracked once again, the loud screech of a seagull wrested him from his wardrobe conundrum. *Oh, fuck it. I'll see what the boys are wearing and then decide.*

With that, Ollie pulled on clean underpants, socks and a T-shirt, slipped back into his tracksuit bottoms and crept up the few steps to his neighbour's landing. Seeing the light under the door and hearing the low hum of music, he paused for a moment. Only now did it occur to him that, like the showroom dummies in Nice 'n' Naughty, his neighbour would also be in mourning. Though he hoped not in the same French maid's outfit or jockstrap. Bette did know Grace. He was certain of that from conversations they'd shared on the stairs. But how close were they? Oh well. There was only one way to find out.

'Helloooo! It's Ollie. Are you decent?' he shouted over the music.

Moments later, an unexpectedly chirpy Bette came to the door.

'Oh, I could never be accused of that, dear!'

Mmmm, not so grief-stricken after all, thought Ollie.

'Sorry to bother you. I can see you're getting ready to go out,' he said, realising from the white face, hair net and fake boobs that his neighbour was already halfway through creating the star of stage that was the drag sensation, Bette Y'Sweet Ass. And judging by the glazed look across her piercing blue eyes, Ollie was pretty sure that wasn't the only thing Bette was halfway through. A suspicion supported a moment later by the open bottle of gin he spied on the cocktail bar in the corner of the lounge. Or had she perhaps been crying? Given the circumstances, both were possible. But then again it could just as easily have been the effect of so many fairy lights strewn on pictures around the room.

'I just wanted to say how sad I was to hear about your friend,' said Ollie.

'Oh, that is kind of you, dear. Thank you. At least I got to say my goodbyes before she…' began Bette, looking upwards and waving her hand in the direction of the ceiling and the walls. Ollie took this to mean, 'before she died' rather than 'before she decorated the lounge'.

'Oh… I didn't realise you…'

'Yes, dear. She's not been well for some time now. When I went on Saturday, I knew it would be the last time I'd see her for a while. So, when the home called this morning… I wasn't surprised,' Bette sniffed, taking a swig from her glass and confirming three things for Ollie. She *had* been crying. She *had* been drinking. And Bette and Grace were more than just acquaintances. Suddenly feeling a little uncomfortable, Ollie decided to change the subject.

'So, you'll be going to the candlelit vigil tonight?' he asked, assuming that was the reason for the transformation.

'Dear God, no. Can't be doing with that dreary old nonsense. Not tonight anyway. Let's save that for the funeral.'

Oh fuck! The funeral!

'Oh yes. Any idea when…'

'Yes, dear. Friday after next. A memorial service at St. Mary's first. Then up to Woodvale Crematorium. But let's not think about that now. I want tonight to be about her life, not her death.'

Result! Not only the date but the venue for the service *and* the funeral too. But what did she mean about 'tonight'?

Was there more? Sensing he was pushing at an open door, he decided to push his luck too.

'Tonight?'

'Yes, dear,' enthused Bette in her 'show must go on' mode. 'At the Queens Arms. We're having a proper knees-up. Been planning it for days. I even let Gracie in on it. She always did hate surprises!'

Caught somewhere between shock and disbelief by his neighbour's bold approach to the dying, Ollie was unsure how to react – but decided to go with the flow.

'Fantastic! What time does it all kick off?' he said, not at all sure that a wake was something you generally 'kicked-off'.

'Oh yes, do come along. Got to keep our spirits up haven't we, dear? In fact,' said Bette, glancing over at the bottle of gin on the counter.

Not waiting for Ollie's answer, the half-dressed – and almost certainly half-cut – drag queen wafted over to the corner of the lounge and poured a finger or two of gin into two tumblers.

'Yes, thank you, if you're sure it's…'

Just then a new song started playing in the background. Or rather it was an old song. Ollie recognised the tune from an 80s romcom his mum used to watch all the time. But he guessed from the crackles coming from the gramophone speaker that this was the original recording from the 60s. The haunting harmonies of two men reverberated around the room, and it seemed to Ollie that Bette had become lost in her *own* thoughts of yesteryear. But just as Ollie thought he was in danger of drowning in the waves of nostalgia lapping around his ears, Bette threw him a lifeline.

'Ice and a slice, dear?'

'Yes please,' enthused Ollie, grabbing hold of Bette's words and dragging himself back into the here and now.

'To Gracie,' announced Bette, clinking their glasses.

'Gracie!' Ollie repeated back.

'Seems like only yesterday we were all together,' said Bette, looking into the distance. At first, Ollie thought he was going to lose her again. But no, that wasn't it. She was looking at something over Ollie's shoulder. Tempted to turn around to see what had caught her attention, he was also keen for her to keep at least one high heel in the present and tried again to drag her back to the matter in hand.

'I just wondered what time it...'

'Ah yes, dear. The wake. Curtain up at nine thirty,' she said, handing him a piece of paper from the coffee table. 'It's all there, dear.'

'Brilliant!' replied Ollie, relieved that his intervention had worked. 'No doubt you'll be giving us a colourful performance tonight.'

'Well, you can *bet your sweet ass* there will be an awful lot of blue!' she shrieked, giving him a knowing wink and waltzing off towards the kitchen.

Sensing he had outstayed his welcome, Ollie put down his half-finished drink, shoved the note in the back pocket of his tracksuit bottoms and got ready to leave.

'Right. I better be off,' he said, making his way into the hall. 'Thanks for the drink. And the info about tonight.'

'My pleasure,' shouted Bette, from the other room. 'Pull the door to when you go, will you, dear?'

'Yes, of course,' replied Ollie over his shoulder. But as he reached for the handle, he couldn't help being distracted by a framed photograph in the hallway where Bette's gaze had been focused a few minutes earlier. In the picture was a boy in his teens with blond hair and piercing blue eyes. Oddly familiar, Ollie wished he could have studied it a little longer. But it was getting late, and he was no closer to deciding what to wear for the vigil. And even more challenging. *Where was he going to get candles from at this time of night?*

Chapter Four

The winner takes it all

As Cameron walked down St. James's Street, he couldn't help but feel just a wee bit pleased with himself. By the time he arrived at the vigil, his obituary had been 'liked' by over five hundred people. The candlelit affair in front of the AIDS memorial on the New Steine had provided him with more than enough sombre photos to stoke his social media engine for a good few hours yet. *The piccy of a seagull perched on top of the statue had got quite a few comments already.* And then there was the inside-track information about the funeral that Ollie had gleaned from Bette earlier on. Well done, Ollie. *Not just a pretty face!*

As his personal trainer, Cameron also had Ollie to thank for something else; his trim figure, honed and shaped during their twice-weekly pre-work workouts. It was how they had become friends in the first place. Though in many ways they were polar opposites, over the last few years, Cameron had grown fond of Ollie's happy-go-lucky approach to life and especially looked forward to his gossipy early morning banter.

Reminded of his friend, Cameron suddenly became aware that he had arrived at the Queens Arms without

Ollie – or indeed, his husband. *Where were they?* Probably still chatting to the laddie that Ollie had introduced him to at the vigil. Turning his gaze back up the hill, Cameron spied his friend's rainbow flag shawl and Alex's *Make America Gay Again* baseball cap amongst the mass of twinkling candles. As he had suspected, the cause of their delay was walking in between them looking slightly bemused by the whole thing. Ah, never one to look a gift horse in the mouth was our Ollie, thought Cameron, fully aware of his friend's eternal search for Mr Right. *Fair enough, I suppose.* Before gay marriages, funerals were to gay singletons what weddings had always been for the straights. As Alex had said earlier while advising Ollie on what to wear to the evening's event. *'I mean, doll, who doesn't look good in black?'* And given where they'd met, there was an outside chance that the strong-jawed skinhead that Ollie was making moon eyes at was more Mr Right than 'mister right now' – the category of men that Ollie usually ended up meeting via the various dating apps he patronised. Certainly, the tattoo of a cherub that Cameron had noticed on the bicep of Ollie's latest conquest seemed to suggest he had a sensitive side. Finally catching Alex's eye in the crowd, Cameron held up four fingers with one hand and made a drinking gesture with the other before entering the pub and pushing his way to the bar.

To kill a little time while he got served, Cameron took stock of what he had learned about Grace's funeral thus far. As well as the date, Bette had revealed that the service was to be at St. Mary's, the huge kirk at the bottom of Upper Rock Gardens. Just a wee hop, skip and a jump away from his and Alex's house in Wyndham Street, so theirs would be the perfect venue for a post-service soirée.

Of course, the most pressing intel was about *this* evening's event. Curtain up at nine thirty, hadn't Bette said?

He glanced at his phone. They were just in time. No sooner had he flashed his mobile over the payment machine at the bar than the house lights dimmed and the sound system switched from some dance track he didn't recognise to a classical one that he did; Handel's *Zadok the Priest.*

How appropriate thought Cameron, for out of the corner of his eye, resplendent in crown and faux-fur collared cape, he saw Bette. The crowd erupted in cheers and wolf-whistles. It helped of course that Bette was accompanied by two musclebound hunks in gold lamé trunks. Even more so when, once on stage, they happily allowed her to give their crown jewels a gentle squeeze. But Bette had one more crowd-pleaser up her sleeve. The dazzling rhinestone-encrusted ballgown that she was wearing beneath her cape. One yank later and the entire ceiling was lit with a glittering firmament of green stars stretching into every corner of the room.

'Fantaaaabulous!' screamed Cameron to Alex, in a volume of camp – and Scots – that surprised even himself.

'Ladies and gentlemen,' announced the DJ from behind the bar. 'The Queens Arms is proud to present your hostess for this evening. Our very own Queen of Tarts. Ahem. Sorry! Our very own Queen of Hearts. The one. The only. Miss Bette Y'Sweet Ass.'

Triggering a second wave of adoration, Bette sank gracefully into her throne and waved regally at her subjects while the spotlight moved onto the dance floor for the DJ to introduce the evening's support acts.

'And also, for your delectation and pleasure this evening… please put your hands together for Miss Jason!'

Renewed applause.

'Keep your hand on your ha'penny for Davina Sparkle.'

More cheering and wolf-whistles.

'And keep your hand on your wallet for Miss Leer Jett.'

Approaching the finale and the spotlight on her once more, Bette rose from her throne and readied herself for the moment the crowd had been waiting for.

'So, boys and girls,' she purred into the mic. 'Are we gonna give Gracie a send-off to remember?'

Like everyone in the bar that night, Cameron knew this was his cue to shout out Bette's well-worn catchphrase. Buoyed up by the heightened emotions of the occasion, he and his fellow mourners did not disappoint.

'You bet your sweet ass we are!' came the reply from the crowd.

'Fucking A. This is gonna be stoatin',' shouted Cameron to his husband. But before Alex could reply, Bette was back on the mic.

'That's right boys and girls. You can bet your sweet ass we are. Save your tears for the memorial.'

A few cheers from the audience.

'Tonight, me and the Queens Arms Girls are going to celebrate the amazing life of Grace Davidson with a selection of old favourites that will lift all our spirits and remind us that, even without our leading lady, the show *will* go on.'

More cheers and wolf-whistles.

'So, in honour of her royal highness, here's a little medley especially for Queen Gracie.' On cue, the music kicked in, and the opening bars of 'No More Tears' began to trickle through the sound system. Time tae lift some o' those spirits, decided Cameron, making his way back to the bar. G&Ts secured, he was about to return to the boys when he heard a familiar voice behind him.

'Miss Cameroon! Miss Cameroon!'

Wincing slightly at this corruption of his name, he was quickly joined by the excitable presence of his friend,

Adam Moxon. Well-built and hirsute, Adam belonged to the fraternity of gay men known as bears. A wee bit older than Cameron – his beard and short-cropped hair already silver in colour – they had first met through work. Adam had once part-owned a social media start-up in London, which he'd sold for a packet before packing it all in and opening a deli-diner on the edge of Queen's Park, a short walk from St. James's Street. His coarse humour, shameless promiscuity and heavy drinking belied a shrewd business mind, and before long, his new venture had also become a roaring success. Cameron had to admit to being just a little bit envious of Adam's escape from adland. And as an antidote to his husband's increasing campery, he also found his brooding masculinity pretty damn hot too.

'How arrrrrrre you?' growled Adam in his thick Northern Irish brogue. It was a moot question since Adam's attention was already elsewhere.

'Who's the hottie with Ollie?' he bellowed, with what seemed to Cameron to be more genuine interest.

'Some fella he met at the vigil. He's called Drew, I think.'

'Drew! Drool more like. Lucky Ollie! Let's go and break 'em up!' Adam cackled. Though knowing Adam's reputation, Cameron suspected he was only *half* joking.

With both of them pushing through the crowd together, a few seconds later they were face to face with the others. Of course, as soon as the usual kisses and greetings were over, the main focus of attention was the new kid on the block.

'So, Drew. What do you think of the show so far?' asked Adam.

'Outstanding!' replied Drew in what Cameron thought was a Welsh accent. 'You boys definitely know how to throw a wake. And Bette is just briiiilliant!' he continued, his accent getting stronger as he did so.

'She's a treasure, that's for sure,' replied Cameron, completing the Celtic trinity.

'Aye. With a big feckin' treasure chest on her too,' slurred Adam, shifting a little bit closer to his prey. Perhaps he had been encouraged by Drew's polite snigger at his double-entendre, thought Cameron. Though knowing that Adam's accent was often quite difficult to decipher, even before several pints of lager, he suspected that Drew's response was out of politeness rather than genuine appreciation of his friend's wordplay. Despite this likely truth, the Irishman continued to make his move.

'Fantastic turnout, too. Especially as it was so last minute. The whole town's gone into shutdown. I even closed the café early today. Out of respect,' said Adam, moving in even further.

When the daggers Ollie threw in Adam's direction did nothing to deter the onslaught, Cameron thought it best to step in.

'Adam owns Moxon's in Queen's Park. You should get Ollie to take you there.'

'Ah! The one that sells *everything but the girl*,' replied Drew, referring to the witty line that Adam had painted on the window in honour of his favourite band.

'I bloody love that place. Especially your full English. Cured a few Sunday hangovers, those sausages have, I can tell you!'

'Thanks, mate. Always good to be complimented on the quality of my meat!' Adam snorted. The fact that Adam rarely worked the Sunday shift at the café not only explained why he hadn't clocked Drew before now – but also why his sausages weren't the only *fresh meat* getting a five-star review that evening.

'Ha. Ha. Very funny,' deadpanned Ollie, making it clear that he, for one, was not amused by Adam's blatant flirting.

In fact, he was not alone. As much as Cameron liked Adam, he didn't always approve of his forwardness with other people's boyfriends – especially as Ollie hadn't even had the chance to call Drew that yet. Accordingly, he made another attempt to stop Adam from pulling a Jolene.

'So, Drew, are you planning on going to the memorial service?' asked Cameron.

'I'm not sure. When is it?'

'Apparently, it's all set for next Friday. At St. Mary's just up the road from here. In fact, we're having a wee do of our own afterwards, if you fancy joining us.'

'Oh yes, you can be Ollie's plus one,' added Alex, picking up the baton on behalf of married couples everywhere in their campaign to encourage singletons to join them in their gilded cages.

'Thanks. I'll see what I've got on at work and…' began Drew.

But before he could finish his sentence, Adam grabbed the baton and was off again. 'So, Drew, what do you do for a living?'

'I'm a mechanic. Got a space at Ditchling Rise Studios.'

'A gay mechanic. Wow, that's so hot.'

But then something miraculous happened. Ignoring Adam's last comment, Drew wrapped his right-arm around Ollie's waist, pulled him in close and pecked him affectionately on his left cheek.

Yes! thought Cameron to himself. One-nil to Ollie. Positions noted, they turned back towards the pub just as Miss Jason and Davina Sparkle began singing 'Thank You for the Music'. Though after Drew's declaration of love, there was only one ABBA song in Cameron's head at that precise moment.

Chapter Five

Done Roman

Tuesday 8th October 2019 – 11am – Bear Road, Brighton

Focused on the promise of a tinkle, a coffee and the organic biscuits she'd bought at a farmers' market during her weekend in the Cotswolds, the last few steps to her front door felt like a homerun to Izzy Pitt. Reaching the zenith, she paused a moment to refamiliarize herself with the spectacular panorama. Indeed, had the final ascent not already done so, the view from the top of one of Brighton's steepest roads would certainly have left her breathless.

In the few seconds it took to retrieve her door keys, Izzy made a bird-like scan of the vista. From right to left, she took in the curved line of white stucco villas known as Round Hill Crescent. Beyond that, the lush green escarpment which marked the edge of the South Downs. And twisting her head around a little further, her eyes fell upon the overgrown forest-like wilderness that was Brighton Borough Cemetery. Not only the final resting place for the town's great and good – and Izzy suspected quite a lot of its mediocre and downright bad – but also the resting place for thousands of species of flora and fauna. So, it was friendly reassurance that Izzy felt when she came face to face with an actual bird staring at her from the cemetery wall opposite the house. And though she had to admit it was unusual to see a seagull this far from the beach, since they were as Brighton as sticks of rock and fish and chips, she concluded that it was a fitting welcome home.

Keys found, seconds later, she was inside. As she stepped over the mail, her eyes were immediately drawn to the headline on the newspaper that sat on top of the mound of letters and magazines.

BRIGHTON ROCKED!

She dropped her rucksack, scooped up the paper and ran upstairs. Of course, she knew exactly why Brighton was rocked. How could she not have done after Cameron's social media post the previous day? How inconvenient of Grace to shuffle off her mortal coil when she was out of town, thought Izzy as she pulled up her combats and flushed the loo. But more importantly, how was she going capitalise on the event before MacIntyre made his next move?

Wrested from these thoughts by her husband slamming the front door, a few minutes later she was luxuriating under the snowy bubbles of a piping hot bath. *Ah... nothing makes one appreciate the trappings of modern life more than a few days under canvas.* Feeling her spirits lifted a little, she reached for the newspaper that she'd placed on the bathroom stool.

'Condolences and flowers began arriving at the home of Grace Davidson yesterday, as news of the death of one of Brighton's most loved residents spread across the city. The UK's first ever transgender MP and former Mayor of Brighton & Hove, Grace passed away peacefully at her care home in Rottingdean aged 83. Emigrating to the UK from Italy after the war, she later moved to New York and then San Francisco, where she worked alongside trail-blazing gay politician, Harvey Milk. Moving to Brighton shortly after his assassination in 1978, Grace opened one of the country's first gay-friendly hotels in the UK and later formed the Kemptown Association of Small Businesses and Hoteliers to give the area's small businesses a voice in the city. Including representatives from several gay businesses, KASBAH was largely responsible for the development of St. James's Street into the gay mecca that it is today. It was not, however, until the AIDS crisis that she began to play a role in issues affecting the wider LGBTIQ+ community. In this era of ignorance and fear, one voice of reason rose above all others. The compassionate and resolute voice of Grace Davidson. Compassionate when she opened up her hotel to gay men who had lost their jobs and homes as a result of the prejudice surrounding the virus. Resolute when she refused to allow opponents to use the disaster to turn back the tide of gay rights and acceptance in the city. A leading campaigner against Clause 28, she organised and spoke at many rallies against the legislation. Building on the experience gained during these dark times, Davidson became a councillor in 1990, aged 55. Representing the ward focused on St. James's Street for 5 years, she was elected to the office of Mayor in 1996 and a year later took the newly created seat of Brighton East Cliff in the 1997 General Election. Though standing as an Independent, she was a key spokesperson on pro-LGBTIQ+ legislation of the period, including the repeal of Section 28 (formerly Clause 28), the equal age of consent, the beginnings of gay marriage legislation and the Gender Recognition Act (2004). Standing down as an MP in 2005, aged 70, she retired to the sheltered housing complex in Rottingdean that she helped set up for LGBTIQ+ senior citizens. As she had no surviving relatives, her estate will be divided between the many charities she supported in her lifetime. As a sign of respect, Brighton & Hove City Council has declared the day of her funeral an official day of mourning. All council employees will be given the morning off, and private businesses are encouraged to follow suit. The service will take place at St. Mary's Church on Friday 18th October at 11am and will be followed by a funeral cortège up to the Woodvale Crematorium via the Old Steine, Ditchling Rise and Bear Road. Mourners who are unable to attend the ceremony can watch the service online at……'

'Eureka!' cried Izzy. She'd found it. The thing that would enable her to steal a march on Cameron. Coming through town, the cortège would drive past their house on the way up to the crematorium's top entrance. It would, therefore, be the perfect venue for a post-funeral gathering. She could barely contain her excitement. But resisting the urge to leap out of the bath, she returned the newspaper to the stool, gently climbed out of the water, and wrapped a towel around herself.

'I'm out, darling,' she cried downstairs, skipping across the landing into their bedroom. Swapping the towel for a kimono and easing her auburn hair into a turban to dry, she made herself comfortable at the dressing-table. Her roots would need doing again soon, she noted. But thanks to her Mediterranean skin, she was confident that she looked younger than her grey hair suggested. So much so that people were often surprised she had a son who was already at college. Reminded of that fact, her eyes fell upon the framed photo of Josh, taken on his 17th birthday. Getting more like his dad every day, she thought to herself, looking at his sparkly brown eyes, freckled cheeks and goofy ears. But while Ken had been rather pale as a teenager, Josh was much darker than his father had been at that age. And then there was his rebellious nature! Like his olive skin, Izzy was convinced that this came from her side of the family. *Take his recent announcement that he was queer, for instance.* Not that him 'coming out' had been a problem. *Surely there were fewer cities in Britain where a parent's claim that 'some of their best friends were gay' was more credible.* It was certainly the case for Izzy and Ken, for not only was her own sister, Maria, a lesbian, but her husband's Aunt Paula, too. In fact, their 'gay best friends' were the reason why Izzy and Ken had moved to Brighton in the first place.

Living and working in London since his early twenties, Ken had visited his aunt in Brighton often over the years. So, when Paula died suddenly in 2017 – single and childless – it wasn't particularly surprising that he'd ended up with her house. What Izzy hadn't expected though, was that rather than selling it, Ken had wanted to up sticks and move into it instead. Perhaps it was the fact that she'd recently turned 50 – or that her sister had already made the move to the city several years earlier – but somehow, she had been persuaded to leave the suburbs of London and set up home in his aunt's old house.

Of course, boasting as it did, one of the UK's most vibrant LGBTIQ+ communities, she now knew why Josh had also been so keen to move to Brighton! But no, the recent announcement about his sexuality had not been a major issue for either Izzy or Ken.

His decision to move in with his boyfriend in the final year of his A-Levels, however! That had not gone down quite so well. Especially with Izzy. *He'd soon tire of doing his own laundry, Ken had tried to reassure her.* But the pile of mail on the doorstep was proof that he had not done so just yet. Though in truth, Izzy knew that it wasn't concerns over his studies that had upset her; he'd also inherited her academic bent and loved college to bits. No, that wasn't the reason. As uncomfortable as it sat with her 'cool mum' image, the source of her objection was having to accept that Josh was becoming his own man. He'd certainly wasted no time making new friends since moving here; the student with whom he now shared a washing machine, for instance! *But then again, hadn't she too experienced a new lease of life since arriving in the city?* The fact was that far from missing her London circle, she found the gaggle of Brightonians she'd met through Maria to be even more fascinating than the friends she'd left behind. Thinking about these new acquaintances suddenly reminded her of the task in hand and of one person in particular; Cameron MacIntyre, the bitchy redhead who clearly saw himself as kingpin of the group and with whom she had already clashed on several occasions since entering his realm. It was obvious that he saw her as competition, even though by London standards she thought she'd been rather low key thus far. But now the house had been purged of Aunt Paula's dated colour schemes and furnishings, the gloves were off, and it was time for the battle royal to commence.

She smiled at the photo of Josh and made a mental note to call him as soon as she had charged her phone. In fact, since it had been dead for the last few hours, he may even have called *her*. Satisfied that it would all come out in the wash – no matter where he ended up doing *his* – Izzy's thoughts returned to her post-funeral gathering.

How quickly it all began to fall into place. She and her guests could watch the service on the telly in the lounge. *So much more comfortable than sitting on those cold, hard pews in St. Mary's*. And then they could watch the *actual* cortège from the lounge window. In fact, if the weather was fine, they could even take the few steps up the hill to the crematorium itself. *Oh, this is going to be great*. Hearing Ken sloshing in the bath, she quickly located her soccasins and made her way downstairs to plan the finer details of her post-funeral gathering. Post. Funeral. Gathering. Just the mere sound of it was delicious to Izzy. And with her head swirling with images of ancient druid rituals, she merrily set up her laptop on the kitchen table. A photo of Grace and a few well-chosen words later and invitations to a ringside seat at the 'funeral of the year' were dropping into the in-boxes of friends, neighbours and work colleagues – all over Brighton.

'Bravo!' she exclaimed, closing the lid of her laptop just as the espresso pot had a hissy fit on the hob. Next job; the mail. And what an interesting pile it was too. In addition to the usual rag, tag and bobtail of bank statements and bills, there was a history magazine, which this month promised a fascinating article about a diary belonging to a nun from Whitby who was being heralded as a medieval Pepys. And then there was Ken's fitness magazine, the plastic outer of which he rarely had the strength to rip open. But the envelope that caught her attention was the one that had all the trademark signs of a party invitation. Handwritten address. Textured paper. Proper stamp.

It was, of course, the much-anticipated invitation to what promised to be the 'housewarming party of the year.' Much-anticipated because the renovation of a former abbey in nearby Rottingdean – that Maria and her wife, Meena, had bought a couple of years back – had been the subject of numerous round-robin emails that Izzy had received from the couple over the last 12 months. Updates on the re-pointing of the medieval brickwork. Bulletins about roof repairs. And most gripping of all, the arrival of the new boiler. Building work, plumbing and carpentry which had, by and large, been done by Maria herself. The fact was that despite their closeness, the two sisters could not have been more different. Isobel, cerebral, bookish; Maria, practical, good with her hands. Isobel, elegant and feminine; Maria, tomboyish and handsome. Even in stature, they had little in common. One tall and willowy, the other short and sturdy. Izzy smiled at the envelope. As much as she loved her sister, she couldn't help but hope that the arrival of the party invitation might also signal an end to the monthly renovation updates. Even more cause for celebration, thought Izzy to herself as she leaned the envelope against the sugar bowl, in preparation for its grand opening. She did not have to wait long.

Coffee percolated and poured, Izzy had just enough time to decant the milk from a plastic carton into the more aesthetically pleasing blue and white jug she had picked up on their trip when she heard the creak of Ken's footsteps on the wooden staircase. Dressed in blue and white pyjamas and sporting his Harris tweed slippers – another souvenir from one of their life-affirming trips into the great outdoors – it was clear to Izzy that he too was enjoying the return to creature comforts. It also struck her how much his outfit reminded her of their new jug, especially with his damp white hair. But she decided to keep the comparison to herself.

'Ahhhhh... civilisation at last,' he said, breathing in the aroma of freshly brewed coffee and throwing the newspaper down on the table. 'Nice article about Grace, don't you think?' From the conversation triggered by Cameron's post the previous day, Izzy knew that Ken was fond of the former MP. As a regular visitor to the city over the years, he was well aware of the high esteem in which she was held by Brightonians and had been genuinely moved by the news of her death. Even so, she decided to keep the plans for her little gathering under her hat for now. Especially as there was the invitation to Maria and Meena's housewarming to open.

'Here you go, darling,' she said, handing him a mug of coffee.

'Gracias, cariña.'

Ignoring this allusion to her native, but rarely spoken first language, Izzy picked up the envelope that had been leaning against the sugar bowl and waved it like a Spanish fan.

'Que hay?' he said, goading her once again.

'Let's see!' replied Izzy, pointedly in English. Proud of the fluency with which she spoke her adopted language, Izzy refused to be drawn into Spanglish, and ignoring Ken's attempt to do so, she deftly slid one of her finely manicured talons under the flap and took out the enclosed card.

'Winter Tableaux Vivants,' she announced, theatrically.

'Winter *Tableaux* what?'

'Tableaux Vivants. Living pictures. You know. Posing for a photograph – in costume.'

'Oh hell. More fancy-dress,' groaned Ken.

Though her husband had once been a bit of a party animal, after his fiftieth birthday, Izzy had noticed a significant drop in his enthusiasm for the social whirl of which she enjoyed being at the centre. Increasingly preferring to spend his weekends in front of the telly with a glass of red, rather than playing prince consort to her Queen Bee, he had even created an acronym to describe the condition. While the scourge of the millennial was FOMO: the Fear Of Missing Out, Ken had proudly told her recently that he was suffering from FOBI: the Fear Of Being Invited. Perhaps he had thought that moving out of London would usher in a less hectic social life. *How wrong he had been!* So, assuming his displeasure about the prospect of having to dress up was just a symptom of his FOBI psychosis, Izzy ignored his distress and continued reading out the invitation.

'Maria and Meena kindly request the company of Isobel & Ken at Coleshill Abbey on Saturday 30th November 2019 at 8pm.'
'Theme: Historical Lovers Through the Ages.'

'Ugh! Who do we have to be *this* time?' sighed Ken, his mood darkening as Izzy scanned through the text.

'Fantastic. They want us to be Antony and Cleopatra!'

'Really?' enquired Ken.

His unexpected change of tone had not gone unnoticed by his wife.

'Why, what?'

'Well, it's just I'm sure I saw a Roman soldier costume in that trunk of Aunt Paula's in the attic.'

'Oh, wow, how interesting,' replied Izzy, raising a brow. The truth was that Izzy had been looking for a reason to rummage through Paula's old things in the attic for quite some time. If it hadn't been for the incessant decorating that had occupied the last 12 months, she would have been up there already. That and Ken's reluctance to disturb memories of his beloved aunt. The fact that he had mentioned the costume was perhaps a sign that he was finally out of mourning and ready to get rid of some of Paula's rubbish at last.

Encouraged by her husband's unexpected enthusiasm for the upcoming housewarming, she suddenly decided that now was a good time to tell him about her hastily arranged gathering. 'I'm glad you are feeling more sociable, cariño, because I'm planning a little party of our own. Just a few friends and neighbours to watch Grace Davidson's funeral cortège…'

'Ah, I wondered why you'd left the paper on the bath stool! *Sneaky!* But I do think we should mark the occasion. She did a lot of good for this city. And I'm sure Aunt Paula would approve. As long as you don't expect me to wear a mourning coat and top hat,' said Ken, for once showing few signs of FOBI. But before she could spill the beans about her post-funeral gathering, the sound of her phone coming back to life in the lounge introduced more pressing tasks.

'Oooh. I better call Maria. Thank her for the invite. And Josh, to tell him we are back from our travels.'

Dropping the invitation into Ken's lap, she wandered off to find her mobile. Though if Ken thought he had been saved from further discussion about the upcoming get-together – he was wrong.

'Bastardo!' screamed Izzy from the lounge. *'Hijo de perra!'*

'What? What? What?' cried Ken, leaping up from his seat and joining her in the front room.

'Ese hombre!' she shouted at him, before realising – from the look on Ken's face – that she had fallen into her native tongue.

'Which man? Who?'

'Who do you bloody think? Cameron-fucking-MacIntyre, of course. That's who. He's just sent me an invite to his *post-service soirée*. Fuuuuuuck!'

Chapter Six

Amazing Grace

Thursday 17th October 2019 – midday –
St. Mary's, Kemp Town

Though he considered himself more spiritual than religious, George was no stranger to the huge Victorian church at the top of St. James's Street. Not only was it the venue for the annual AIDS concert at which George – as Bette Y'Sweet Ass – often performed, but it was also the place from where he'd said goodbye to many of his friends over the years. In fact, given the cause of so many of those farewells, it was fitting that St. Mary's was where, in a few days' time, Brighton would come to pay their respects to the person who had perhaps done more than anyone to support the community through those dark times. The reason for George's visit today was, of course, to discuss Grace's funeral. He was there to make the final arrangements for the service with the church verger, Stephen Tindale; a gentleman in his early forties, who, with his pudding basin haircut and round spectacles, always reminded George of a middle-aged beatnik. Also, the organist and choirmaster at St. Mary's, it was Stephen's baritone voice that greeted George as he stepped into the church.

'Benito! Nooooooooo!' yelled Stephen in the direction of the baptismal font, which at that precise moment was getting a christening of its own from a scraggy-haired fox terrier who was known to all and sundry as Mr Ben. Having met the dog on several occasions, George knew that hearing shouts of *Il Duce* could mean only one thing.

'Miss Blythe! Miss Blythe!' cried Stephen, down to the other end of the church. 'Mop and bucket. Quick sticks please!'

Being rather short-sighted, the figure in the chancel was little more than a blur to George, but he recognised the name immediately. In fact, once upon a time, he and Jane Blythe had been quite friendly. He seemed to recall she'd had a bit of a thing for a boyfriend of his. Until she realised that she was barking up the wrong tree! But that was a million years ago, and the only thing she and George had in common these days was a postcode and their age. Of course, living in the same neighbourhood for half a century, their lives had criss-crossed every now and again. Before retiring, Jane had been a midwife at the Royal Sussex County Hospital up the road, so George had seen her several times over the years; especially during the 80s and early 90s, when he seemed to spend half his life there. But while it was highly unlikely that Jane knew nothing of his transformation into local celebrity, Bette Y'Sweet Ass, as far as their social spheres were concerned, they may as well have inhabited different planets. And as for *her* transformation! Seeing her close up, George found it hard to believe that the tired-looking woman in floral apron and headscarf, scuttling up the aisle with a mop and bucket, had once been the happy-go-lucky girl that he had shared one memorable summer with a lifetime ago.

'Thank you, Miss Blythe. He's very sorry, aren't you, Mr Ben?' said Stephen, grabbing the dog's leash and turning to George.

'So sorry, Mr Gibbons. Won't be a sec. Let's go to my rooms at the back. Time for Mr Ben's afternoon nap!'

Fortunately for George and Jane Blythe, the commotion caused by Mr Ben spared them the embarrassment of a formal re-introduction, and they simply nodded to each other as they passed in opposite directions down the middle of the church. Safely seated in Stephen's flat built onto the back of the church, the purpose of the meeting could begin.

'*Amazing Grace!*' said George, waving the *wish-list* he'd retrieved from the blue box on the morning of Grace's passing.

'Brilliant!' enthused Stephen, setting down a tray of tea things and cake on the kitchen table.

'Of course, when she wrote the *wish-list* in the early 90s, she had no idea how her life was going to turn out. We'd just said goodbye to yet another friend, and we both did one as a way of dealing with the horror of it all.'

'Oh gosh, she wasn't…' interrupted Stephen.

'No, I just think, you know, that whole thing with Harvey Milk. Being there when it happened. Well not actually *there*, but in town when…'

'Oh yes, the gay rights campaigner in San Francisco who was assassinated.'

'Yes. Well, it shook her up quite a bit. Obviously. And when she became more well known, speaking at rallies and being interviewed on TV. Being more in the public eye. Well, knowing what had happened to Harvey. It's bound to make you a bit jittery, isn't it?'

Sensing he had veered off the point a little, George paused a moment to collect his thoughts. 'So, anyway, what I'm saying is, when she wrote it, all those years ago, I think she meant it as a bit of a joke. I mean, with everything going on, you had to find things to laugh about, else you'd just end up crying all the time.'

'Oh, I see. But even so, I think it's very fitting. I mean, she was amazing, wasn't she?' said Stephen, adding milk to George's tea. 'And what's more, I already know that one! Did it at the AIDS concert last year. Or was it 'Hallelujah'? Never mind. I know, I know it. Let's run through it in a mo. And you'll be singing it as Bette, I hope. With the gay choir behind you, you'll bring the house down. Not literally, of course!' he laughed loudly.

'And what else is on her *wish-list*?' said Stephen, removing the marzipan off a piece of Battenberg cake and feeding the sponge to Mr Ben.

'Well. Cremated, not buried, as you know. And…' began George, passing the *wish-list* across the table for Stephen to digest for himself.

'She wants the cortège to be led by a *Ferrari?*' said Stephen, slightly bemused. 'And requests that it takes the Ditchling Rise route up to the crematorium. Well, that shouldn't be too difficult. Odd request, though.'

'Perhaps she wanted one last look at Preston Park. You know how much Grace loved a party!' replied George, referring to the city's popular Pride festival which took place there every August.

'Yes, that makes sense,' said Stephen, blindly feeling for the marzipan he'd denied Mr Ben as he once again became absorbed in the memo from the grave. 'And 'He Who Would Valiant Be' for the finale. *La la-la la la-la-la lah… to be a pilgrim…*' continued Stephen, singing the chorus to the hound at his feet.

'Always good to end on one that everyone knows. Especially as it's being filmed. Don't want to have a load of goldfish singing rhubarb rhubarb… like an episode of

Songs of Praise. More cake? Miss Blythe makes a mean Battenberg. Doesn't she, Mr Ben?'

Just then, as if she had heard her name, Miss Blythe popped her head around the kitchen door.

'Ah, speak of the devil!' announced Stephen, much to the obvious distress of the old woman.

'Sorry to interrupt, Stephen, but the vicar wants you right away. It's the Order of Service for Miss Davidson. There's been a terrible mix-up…'

Sensing an issue of some importance, Stephen jumped up from the table and hurried off in the direction of the chancel, where given the angry voice that George heard next, was where the vicar was already waiting.

'Bother and buggeration, Stephen! What are we going to do now?'

Chapter Seven

God save our gracious screen

'At what point did memorial services merge with drive-in movie night?' joked Cameron, staring at the huge screen that had been erected in front of the chancel.

'I blame Sir Elton and that song he did for Princess Di,' giggled Alex.

'Oh no… don't. Me mam was in bits,' said Drew.

'And don't forget young Tony Blair. I quite fancied him actually.'

'No way!' cried Ollie, shocked by Alex's confession.

'Ach, you wouldnae believe it, but back then he was incredibly popular. Couldn't put a foot wrong,' said Cameron.

'Yep. Still believed that *things could only get better*,' sang Alex.

'Yeah, right. And look how well that turned out,' said Drew, abruptly bringing that particular line of chat to a close.

Searching for a change of subject, Cameron reached inside his jacket for his opera glasses and focused his attention back on the screen. *Oh God. How funny.* On closer inspection, what had appeared to be a screen, was, in fact, four bedsheets. More than that, it seemed that one had sneaked past the hanging committee with a stain that looked more than just a little bit like the Mona Lisa. But before he could share his discovery…

'Oh look, there's Stephen,' shouted Alex, waving furiously in the direction of the verger, dressed in black robes and distributing hymn books to the crowds of mourners squeezed into the pews. Spotting them amongst the congregation, Stephen's face lit up, and he made his way over.

'Soooo pleased you could make it. I've been practising all week, so you better join in,' he garbled at them until Cameron managed to draw his attention to the stain.

'Oh God. I know. Those eyes have been following me around all morning. Hope she doesn't put me off. Especially in front of all these people. Can you believe how packed it is! Had to dig this lot out from the cellar,' huffed Stephen, handing Cameron a pile of tatty old hymn books from an even tattier old cardboard box.

'Sorry about the whiff. If the newspaper they were wrapped in is right, the last time they saw the light of day was Churchill's funeral!'

'Jeez. Are you sure they didn't bury him in them!' said Cameron, catching a noseful of the aforementioned odour as he took one and passed the rest down the line. 'Aren't the hymns usually in the Order of Service?'

'I know. I know. Big fu… mix-up at the printers,' replied Stephen, correcting himself just in time. 'Hence the hymn books instead. We've had to put two lots of numbers up too. One for our usual set and one for this lot,' he said, pointing to the wooden hymn board which had two columns of numbers: one headed 'new' and the other headed 'old'.

'You lot are all *old!*'

'Nice to see you too!' quipped Alex, raising a giggle from all except Stephen, who seemed at that moment to be looking for someone in the crowd.

'Sorry, chaps. Vicar's making his way to the pulpit. It must be time. Gotta go,' said Stephen, turning away and disappearing – in body, if not yet in spirit.

'Who, *or what,* was that?' demanded Drew, utterly thrown by the last two minutes.

'That's our friend Stephen,' chirped Ollie.

'He's the church organist and...' began Alex before being interrupted by Adam appearing at the end of their pew.

'And he's got a feckin' massive organ! Aaaaaaargh!'

The Irish bear was in the building.

'Budge up, ladies,' Adam chided, squeezing himself in on the end.

'Shhhhhh. It's about to start,' chastised Cameron, noting that the stain of Mona Lisa on the bedding had been swapped for an aerial view of St. James's Street and the funeral cortège led by what appeared to be a red Ferrari. How odd, thought Cameron. But there was no time to mention it as seconds later Stephen's aforementioned instrument began girding its pipes for Chopin's Sonata Op.35.

But if he thought these dulcet funereal tones would temper Adam's behaviour, he was to be disappointed. No sooner had the music begun than the image on the screen cut to a live feed of the coffin being carried into the church on the shoulders of eight pallbearers from a local gay rugby club; known as much for their buff bodies and tight-fitting rainbow coloured shorts as they were for their prowess on the playing field. Showing less flesh than was usually the case, nevertheless, their snug black suits left little to the imagination. So little, in fact, that when they entered the church a few moments later, Adam was unable to resist filming their buttocks on the way past.

Thankfully, Grace and the boys made it to the chancel unscathed, and the vicar was able to carry out his duties without any heckling from the back. In fact, once the service began, even Adam was kowtowed by the moving speeches given by some of Brighton's most respected residents, including the current mayor and two local MPs. And most heartfelt of all was the tribute from Bette, who led a local gay choir in a rousing rendition of 'Amazing Grace'. After that, there wasn't a dry eye in the house, and even Cameron found himself wiping away a tear or two. Not particularly comfortable with such public displays of emotion, it was a relief to discover that the final hymn of the service was the upbeat classic, 'He Who Would Valiant Be.' Yet this was not all that he found.

Locating the old favourite in the mildewed hymn book that Stephen had given him, Cameron's heart began beating a little faster. *Oh, my word, what have we got here?* Wedged between the pages of hymn 192, there was an old envelope with what appeared to be a letter inside it.

Careful not to draw attention to his discovery, he slid the yellowing paper out of the envelope and cast his eye over the handwritten note. If seeing the envelope had got his heart racing, when he saw what was written on the page itself, he could barely contain his excitement. Fortunately for Cameron, he didn't have long to wait. A couple more verses of *'...to be a pilgrim'* later and he and Adam were leading the charge out of the church and down to Wyndham Street.

'No sign of the lassies today?' said Cameron, referring to Adam's friend Meena and her wife, Maria, sister of Izzy Pitt.

'No. Bit of a hike from Rottingdean, maybe?'

'Or perhaps they've gone to Bottomless Pitt's 'do-dah' instead,' said Cameron, using the nickname he had come up with for Izzy, in reference to her lanky figure.

'Ah yes, the "gathering"!' laughed Adam.

It was an open secret that Izzy was hosting a counter-event that day, so Cameron was certain that several of those making their way to his soirée had received Izzy's email. Adam included. But he also knew that, as family, Maria and Meena would have been given a three-line whip to attend Izzy's affair.

'Aye, I got the memo! Sounded a bit macabre, to be honest. Besides which, I'd already said yes to you. In any case, I saw Meena and Maria just last week.'

Adam and Meena went back years. They'd known each other as children and had shared a flat together when they first moved to Brighton; Adam to escape the rat race, Meena to flee her rat of a husband.

'They've asked me to do the catering for their housewarming, in fact.'

'Oh yes, the Tableaux Vivants. Who did they want you to be? Narcissus wasn't it?'

'Aye. Feckin' bitches. Maria's idea, I bet.'

'Quite flattering really,' replied Cameron, not believing a word of it.

'Aye. But where am I gonna find someone as gorgeous as me as my plus one.'

Jeez! The girls were closer to the mark than they knew, thought Cameron as they reached his house.

'Shame they couldn't make it today though,' he said, putting the key in the lock and opening the front door. Once inside, he couldn't contain his excitement anymore.

'Especially considering what I've just found!'

Cameron pulled out the envelope from his inside pocket and held it in front of Adam's face with both hands.

'Where the feck…' began Adam, scrutinising the old envelope.

'Tucked into the rancid old hymn book that Stephen gave me.'

'Jaysus. Old is right. Postmark says 1965,' noted Adam, pointing at the black circle stamped on the silver image of a young Queen Elizabeth.

'Yeah, I know. But more than that, I'm pretty sure the letter inside mentions Meena and Maria's new place in Rottingdean,' replied Cameron, loving being in the spotlight.

'What? Coleshill Abbey? Nooooo!'

'Yes. And that's not all.'

'Come on then!' growled Adam, grabbing at the envelope with his bearlike paws. But he wasn't nearly quick enough.

'Hold your horses, doll. Let's get a wee drinkie down us first,' replied Cameron, returning the envelope to the safety of his jacket pocket. The big reveal needed an audience. And after all those hymns, Cameron suspected that Adam would be in need of a drink.

'Aye, good plan. Me mouth thinks me throat's been cut!' conceded Adam, temporarily distracted by the promise of alcohol.

'Fancy a Glemonade?' said Cameron over his shoulder, as he led Adam down the stairs to the basement.

'Glemonade? What the feck's that?'

'Gin and lemonade. It's something we're trying out for the launch of a new gin. Well, an old gin actually. Rakewell's Gin. A campaign I'm pitching for in New York next week. We're targeting the relaunch at millennials, who, according to our research, prefer lemonade to tonic water.'

'Not keen on the quinine, eh?'

'Exactly!' agreed Cameron, impressed with Adam's witty riposte – for once. *I'll have to write that one down.* But there was no time to hunt for pen and paper for the relative calm was suddenly shattered by the sound of Alex and the other guests noisily making their way through the house. That being the case, Cameron emptied a bottle of lemonade into a jug of gin and ice and made his way to the patio to try out the new cocktail on his unsuspecting focus group. Having been incarcerated in self-imposed silence for the last hour and a half, the small crowd was fizzing with conversation and gossip, especially when word got around about Cameron's discovery in the church. But just as Cameron was about to gather the guests together for the big reveal, he heard a familiar cry in the hallway.

'Benito! Nooooo!'

Stephen and his cantankerous old fox terrier had arrived. And the yapping and the sound of claws being scraped along floorboards most likely signalled a canine-related mishap of some kind. As verger, Stephen was not involved in the religious part of the service and had held back to make sure the church was secure. Hearing the commotion, Cameron made his way to the front of the house.

'Stephen. So glad you could make it,' said Cameron, greeting the verger with a beaming smile – and a mop and bucket. 'Come and join us on the patio. Bet you need a drink after all that Chopin!'

'You're not wrong there, dear boy. I'm spitting feathers,' said Stephen, giving the floor a cursory wipe with the mop and following Cameron downstairs. Of course, with the service over and the cortège already up in Izzy's neck of the woods, by the time Stephen had entertained everyone with tales of Mona Lisa's wandering eyes and Mr Ben's recent incident with the baptismal font, the crowd was on the hunt for new news, and it wasn't long before Cameron's recent discovery was the main topic of conversation again.

So, after making sure everyone was sitting, standing or leaning comfortably, Cameron clinked his tumbler with a spoon to get their attention. The crowd sufficiently hushed, he dramatically extracted the letter from its envelope and began...

Georgie boy,

Hope this gets to you in time. Everything's sorted for the 5th. Mancini's hired some old tower nr. Rottingdean. What's left of an old abbey he reckons. Bags of atmos. It's in the back arse of beyond, but there's lecky and water. Reckons it's more private than the usual place. And we can do some outside shots too. He's got a fancy new camera and Paula's borrowed a load of clobber from work. He's even letting me have some wheels for the weekend. Meet us outside Duke's at 6pm. I've missed you rotten this week. Can't wait to get you on your own. Hope you like the photo of us all on Paula's Birthday. Meant to give it you ages ago. Bit squiffy, methinks!

Cameron looked up at his audience and paused for the dramatic finish.

'Wait for it...' he teased. '*All my love... Jack!*'

He couldn't have been more pleased by the effect of his showstopper.

'Oh Em Gee. A love letter!' cried Ollie.

'More than that...' roared Adam. 'It's a feckin' *gay* love letter!'

'From 1965 – according to the postmark!' added Cameron, bathing in the reflected glory of his find. 'But that's not all.' He re-read the line about the abbey. '*Old tower. Derelict abbey. Rottingdean.* It's got to be Meena and Maria's new place, hasn't it? They were meeting at Coleshill!'

'Jaysus! What do you think they were doing there?' asked Adam, grabbing the letter off Cameron and scanning it for the tiniest morsel of a clue. 'Look! Duke's. That has to be the cinema, doesn't it?'

As the oldest cinema in continuous use in the country, the Duke of York's Picture House next to Preston Park held a special place in the hearts of Brightonians, and the mere mention of this proud institution triggered a flurry of knowing nods.

'It was definitely there in the sixties,' confirmed Cameron. 'In fact, if Georgie and Jack were in their twenties or thirties back then, they'd only be in their 70s or 80s now.'

'Only!' shrieked Alex from behind him. *Mmmmm, someone's been hitting those Glemonades!* thought Cameron. But before he could throw his husband one of his disapproving looks, Drew picked up the theme.

'What about the photograph mentioned at the end?'

'That's all there was, I'm afraid,' said Cameron.

'That's a shame,' Drew continued. 'Unlikely we'd recognise any of 'em anyways. Though there might be a record of people who've lived at this address,' he said, holding the envelope Cameron had left on the garden table. *Bugger!* He'd been so focused on delivering Brighton's answer to *Brokeback Mountain,* he'd forgotten all about the envelope!

'Feck! Read it out! Read it out!' cried Adam excitedly.

'Mr G. Gibbons… Number 8…' But no sooner had Drew said the name than Ollie stepped forward and grabbed the envelope from him.

'Gibbons? George fucking Gibbons? Holy fucking fuck!'

'What is it? Do you know him?' asked Cameron.

'You bet your sweet ass I do. In fact, we all do! It's Bette. George Gibbons is Bette!'

Just then, as if to underline the dramatic discovery, Cameron felt something cold splatter on the back of his head.

'Aaaaaargh! Fuck you! Ye beady-eyed beaky bastard!' he cried, looking up at the sky.

Chapter Eight

Billet-doux

Since meeting Drew at the AIDS memorial, Ollie had become quite smitten with his handsome mechanic. They'd been on a few dates and filled each other in on their previous relationships. Admittedly, Ollie had been more economical with the numbers after finding out that Drew could count his exes on one hand. *It was good to have some secrets though, wasn't it?* Besides which, most of Ollie's exes were no more than one-night stands and should more accurately be described as *'whys'*. Why the fuck did I get so drunk? Why do I attract so many nutters? Why didn't I block him? No. It was definitely worth keeping shtum on actual numbers if it meant keeping hold of Drew. But did *Drew* want to keep hold of *him*? It certainly looked promising. For one thing, he'd accepted the invitation to join Ollie at Meena and Maria's housewarming. Wasn't even put off by the tableaux vivant thingamabob. *Who were they supposed to be again? Oscar Wilde and some bloke called Bosie was it?* After a bit of digging around online, Ollie knew it was going to be hard for a mixed-race boy to pull off either of the two looks, but the fact that Drew had agreed to be his 'plus one' to an event that was still a month away. *That had to be a good sign, didn't it?* Hearing the front door open and close below, Ollie was jolted from pleasant thoughts of Drew being a *longer*-term 'plus one' and reminded that he had more detective work to do upstairs. And 'lost property' to return!

Who'd have thought it! His geriatric neighbour, the subject of someone's desire. *George Gibbons – you old devil!* Certainly, the discovery of the love letter had confirmed something that Ollie's generation didn't like to acknowledge about the elderly. They had a past. And worst of all, it involved sex. Despite the discovery of these unsavoury facts, Ollie was keen to get some answers. Who were these ghosts from the old man's past? And what were they doing at Coleshill Abbey all those years ago? Like a moth to an old flamer, Ollie rubbed some aftershave into his five o'clock shadow, slipped on his trainers and made his way upstairs.

'Hello. Anyone home?' said Ollie, standing on the landing outside George's flat.

'Give it a push. It's not locked,' came the voice from beyond.

Opening the door, Ollie came face to face with the boy in the framed photograph that he'd noticed on his last visit. Locking eyes with the young man staring back at him, on closer inspection, he discovered that it was, in fact, the cover of an old magazine. The title he didn't recognise. But the boy? There was definitely something familiar about him. Ollie made a mental note to ask George about him another time. Right now, he had bigger fish to fry. So, putting thoughts of the picture to one side, he followed the voice into the lounge.

To Ollie's great relief, given the circumstances, Bette was clearly having a night off. Sitting comfortably in an armchair, his neighbour looked no different from any other seventy-year-old man relaxing at home of an evening; with the exception perhaps of the traces of blusher and eyeliner that he never quite managed to remove from the folds of his wrinkles. Noticing the remnants of yesterday's make-up on George's face, Ollie was suddenly reminded of Bette's performance at the service, and forgetting the letter, began babbling like a starstruck fan.

'Oh God. You were incredible. We were right at the back, but on an aisle, so we got a great view of the stage. Your 'Amazing Grace' was… amazing. And the gay men's choir, too. The acoustics in the church were out of this world. I bet Grace would have loved it.'

'Oh. I'm sure she did, dear. But are you sure that's what you wanted to see me about?' said George, pointing at the envelope in Ollie's hand.

'Oh yes… sorry. It's this!' said Ollie, passing it over.

The old man reached into his top pocket for his glasses, removed the letter from the envelope and read the contents of the yellowing notepaper. Ollie waited nervously. What if George had simply said, *'Oh thank you, dear, I wondered where I'd put that,'* as if he were acknowledging the return an old brolly or a favourite scarf? But Ollie needn't have worried. He could see from his neighbour's reaction that this was not going to be the case. As George's eyes fell upon the letter, they took on the same glazed look they had on the night of Grace's passing. Adopting what his mother often referred to as her 'bedside manner', Ollie sat down in the chair next to him. Placing the letter in his lap, George carefully removed a handkerchief from the sleeve of his cardigan and dabbed his eyes, releasing the woody scent of eau-de-cologne as he did so. The next few seconds felt like an eternity until finally…

'Where on *earth* did you find this?' said George.

'An old hymn book,' replied Ollie, hugely relieved that his neighbour was indeed the owner of the letter.

'An old hymn book?'

'Yes, ancient!'

'Careful, dear.'

'Sorry, I didn't…' began Ollie, before changing tack. 'What I meant was. Yesterday. At the service. You saw how many people wanted to pay their respects…'

'Standing room only!'

'Yes. Well. They had to bring up some extra hymn books from the cellar. And this was in one of them. Our friend Stephen, the verger, said that he thought they'd not been used since Winston Churchill's funeral. Well, the one they had at St. Mary's to coincide with the big one in London.'

'Ooh, Grace would have loved that. As popular as Churchill!'

'Though apparently they wouldn't have been needed at all if the Order of Service booklets had turned up on time…'

'Oh God! I know all about that!' said George, rolling his eyes. 'What a kerfuffle. I was there when they opened the box on the afternoon before the funeral. The printers had only gone and sent the wrong leaflets!'

'Order of Service for someone else's funeral?'

'Not quite!' said George, pursing his lips. 'Menus. Orders of Service for a Chinese Restaurant!'

'Noooooo!' shrieked Ollie, barely able to disguise his delight. *Stephen had kept that bit quiet!*

'Yes. And far too late by then to do a swap. Vicar was furious!'

'I bet. That's one customer you don't want to mess around!' said Ollie looking upwards.

'Ha! Exactly!'

Sensing a warmth between them, Ollie wondered if George would be willing to share more than a joke with him.

'The thing is…' he began. 'The people mentioned in the letter. I just wondered… what happened to them? They all sound like such characters!'

Ollie knew from their chats on the stairs that George was never more than a few steps away from memory lane, so he decided he was on fairly safe ground.

'Yes, dear. You could say that!' said George, removing his spectacles. 'Mmmmm… let me think. Mancini. I couldn't say. We lost touch shortly after that trip to Rottingdean. But the other two. Gone, I'm afraid.'

'Oh, I am sorry,' replied Ollie, echoing what his mother always seemed to say in these situations.

'Paula. A friend of ours who used to work at the Theatre Royal. She passed away fairly recently. Year before last, I think. I used to bump into her very occasionally around town. But we moved in different circles. And as for Jack. He's been dead for over 50 years. Car accident. Not long after he wrote this, in fact. Somewhere between here and the place mentioned in the letter. Coleshill Abbey it was called. Though there wasn't much left of the abbey by then. Just an old tower and a log-shed.'

'Yes!' exclaimed Ollie, causing George to look up at him, a little startled. 'I mean, yes, that's what we thought,' he added more sensitively.

'We?' said George, clearly shocked by the suggestion that Ollie hadn't been the only one to have read the letter. But seeing no reason to reveal the true number of grubby fingers that had been through George's dirty laundry the previous afternoon, Ollie decided to pick up the previous thread instead.

'Friends of ours bought Coleshill last year. Well, what's left of it, anyway. We felt sure there couldn't be that many ruined abbeys in the area.'

'Oh, I see,' replied George. 'Well, I hope it's a bit more homely than it was back then.'

'You lived there?' asked Ollie, homing in on the word *homely*. 'With this Jack?'

'Not lived exactly. But we used to go there quite a bit. Of course, it was all very hush-hush back then.'

'So, you and Jack…' said Ollie, almost whispering.

'Ha. Thought you'd invented it, did you?' said George with a smile.

'I'm sorry, I …' began Ollie, embarrassed by the thought of his neighbour doing *it*.

'Oh, we were never as in your face as you boys are these days. With me, it was obvious. Not quite so much in your face, as written all over it,' laughed George. 'But Jack. You'd never have known. Tough he was. Had to be. Youngest of five boys.'

'And handsome too I bet! I'd love to see a photo.' If the boy in the frame was the infamous Jack, this would be the ideal moment for George to reveal his identity, thought Ollie.

'So would I, dear. I used to have lots. But they were all destroyed,' said George, shaking his head.

'Destroyed?'

'Yes, dear. In a fire at the abbey. Not long after Jack's…' George's words trailed off into nowhere for a few seconds before he found his voice again. 'Oh well. Thank you again for returning my letter, dear.'

Ollie decided it was a signal that the interview was over.

'You're welcome,' he replied, taking the hint and making his way to the door. 'I'm just sorry there was no photo with the letter,' he added, when they were both in front of the framed magazine cover. *Who was the boy in the picture?* Not Jack, it seemed. *Assuming George was telling the truth about the fire!* But it was certainly where his gaze had fallen the other evening when he'd been reminiscing about the good old days. Ollie was sure of that – at least.

'Yes, that is a shame. Oh well, as long as he's still in here,' said George, touching his head and closing his eyes. 'In fact, I can see him now. In his motor, beeping his horn at me outside Duke's. Silly sod!'

'Oh yes, the cinema,' said Ollie. 'I love that old place.'

'Oh no, dear. Not the cinema. Duke's Garage. On Ditchling Rise. Mancini used to own it. It's where Jack worked.'

'Oh, I see,' said Ollie, stepping back into the landing.

'Yes. Anyway, thank you for the letter, dear.'

With that, George gently closed the door, leaving Ollie alone on the stairwell just as the light in the communal hall timed out.

'Duke's Garage!' said Ollie to himself; enlightened, but also in the dark.

Chapter Nine

Twinkle, twinkle little star

**Friday 5th February 1965 – 6.15pm –
Duke's Garage**

Beeeeeeep, beeeeeep!

Hearing the car horn, George folded the newspaper behind which he'd been hiding and started walking to the Morris that had just pulled up on the other side of the road. As he got closer, a young man with slicked-back hair and sticky-out ears thrust his head out of the window and wolf-whistled in his direction.

'Cooie! Feely omi with the dolly corybungus!' shouted the boy, camply. 'Vada the eek on her. Dilly boy if ever I saw one!'

'Bloody hell, Jack!' growled George, marching around to the other side of the car and quickly getting in. Removing the debris from the front seat – a small blue lunch box and flask – he plonked his *corybungus* down and turned his *eek* to the driver.

'What? Can't I pay my *feely omi* a compliment?' said Jack, cheekily; his pale brown eyes sparkling with mischief and a big grin stretching across his freckle-dusted face.

'Compliment! Since when was calling your boyfriend a rent-boy, a compliment?'

'Dilly boy with a *nice bum* I said! Besides which, I don't reckon they speak much Polari round here, do you?'

Ignoring the likely truth that no one in earshot would have understood a word of the secret gay language he and Jack sometimes talked, George first looked over his shoulder to acknowledge the other passenger in the car – their friend Paula – and then twisted his head back to face the windscreen. Taking the hint, Jack turned the key in the ignition and – like his namesake in the song – proceeded to hit the road…

Once past the racecourse on the edge of the Downs, George could hold it in no longer. One… two… three…

'You're such a cock. You really are. You know I have relatives who live round your gaff. Do you want us to get caught?'

'Not 'arf. Just to see the look on their faces!' cackled Jack, not at all thrown by this outburst. 'Gorgeous Georgie Gibbons getting into a car with another man. What a waste! All that money spent on acting classes, too.'

'Could have been the next Tommy Steele, you know!' added Paula.

'Yeah, yeah, you're hilarious. Real end-of-the-pier stuff. I'll let the Palace Theatre know you're free,' said George, rolling his eyes.

'We're not free, sweet'art,' shrieked Paula in her usual Cockney. Though why she insisted on talking this way was a mystery to George. He knew for a fact she had grown up in Worcestershire and would have needed whale-like sonar to have had any chance of hearing the Bells of Bow on the day of her birth. But since no one ever challenged her on it, to all intent and purposes, she was as Cockney as jellied eels.

'We'd top the bill, Georgie boy. C'mon, Jack, let's have a sing-song.'

'Good idea. Get us in the party mood,' agreed Jack, turning on the transistor radio he'd picked up from the garage.

Not quite ready to agree to a thaw in relations, George continued to give Jack the silent treatment and tried to make eye contact with Paula instead. Glancing up at the rear-view mirror he could see she had been at her hair with the bottle again. Always kept short, the recently applied bleach made her look even more butch than usual. Proper little modette she was these days. She'd even got herself one of those fishtail parkas that were all the rage in Brighton at the minute. Exhausted from trying to hold a conversation from the back, Paula had sunk into the blankets and clothing piled around her and begun singing to the song that was crackling out of the radio. As it happened, an instrumental called 'Green Onions' requiring only the barely tuneful repetition of 'de-de… der-der-der-der… de!'

'Yeah, I bet the Beatles are shitting 'emselves,' cried George, triggering a fit of giggles from all three of them. It was a good sign. Hostilities over, the chatter turned to the upcoming weekend. And there was a good deal to discuss. There would be the box of costumes and props that Paula always managed to beg and borrow, but George suspected rarely returned, from her day job as wardrobe assistant at the Theatre Royal.

'It's all military shit this time,' cried Paula from the back. 'Looks like someone's privates will be on parade this weekend,' she sniggered.

'How long have you been waiting to say that?' howled Jack.

'As long as it's not more of that cowboy shit again,' added George.

'Yeah, right! You bloody loved it when I tied you to that totem pole, Georgie boy. Rock hard, you were!' cried Jack.

'Oh, shut up!' said George. It was true though, he had enjoyed being tied up, and the memory caused him to shift in his seat. Embarrassed, he racked his brains for a change of subject. 'Can't wait to see those whistles from Filk'ns,' said George, referring to some old suits Jack's boss was throwing out that he'd bought from a trendy boutique in the North Laine. Even though the shop had recently shut down, it still held a fascination for the boys, for if the gossip – that is to say Paula – was to be believed, the couple of queens who used to run it offered more than just a snazzy line in Italian threads.

'They'd measure your inside leg – even if you were only buying a tie!' guffawed Paula. Buoyed up by this and similar gems of wisdom from the back seat, the time flew by and before long they were turning onto the pot-holed track they hoped would lead them to the old ruin.

'Look!' cried George, pointing at two flickering lights hovering like eyes in the darkness that had enveloped them in the last half an hour.

'That's it. Mancini said to look out for the windows,' cried Jack. 'And there's his Daimler!' he added, pulling up alongside his boss's car and turning off the headlights of the Morris. Aside from the light coming from the windows of the tower, it was pitch black.

'Wow! Look at the stars, Jack. Aren't they something?'

'God yeah. Amazing,' agreed Jack, resting his head on George's shoulder. But what George thought really was amazing, was the effect the night sky appeared to be having on his boyfriend. While he knew that Jack had a romantic side, it was unusual for him to show it in public. Perhaps he'd forgotten Paula was there? Or maybe he really was starstruck?

'Oh, get a room,' said a voice from the darkness behind them.

But before George could chastise Paula for ruining the moment, Jack turned his head and kissed him full on the lips.

'Ew! Leave it out, you two. I need a piss.'

No chance of Jack forgetting she was in the car now!

Moment properly ruined, Jack pulled away from George and opened his door. Once out of the car, he grabbed a bag and some blankets from the back seat and led the way towards the flickering cat's eyes. Just then the door of the tower swung open, casting a beam of light down towards the three of them and silhouetting Jack's boss in the doorframe.

'Sbrigati, ragazzi!' cried out the figure. 'Sbrigati, sbrigati!'

'Oh good, he's made spaghetti,' whispered Paula.

'You daft mare. It means *get a wiggle on, fellas*. It's one of his catchphrases,' explained Jack, behind a large pile of blankets. 'Yes, Boss. Sbrigati. Sbrigati,' he shouted as he ran towards the tower. As Jack had predicted, there was no homemade pasta. But there was a bottle of red wine waiting for them on the kitchen table.

'Benvenuto a Coleshill Abbey!' announced Mancini, once they were through the door. 'How's the Morris, Jack? No prangs I hope.'

'Good as new, Boss. Good as new.'

'I'll take your word for it. But let's not talk motors. We're not at the garage now. Grab yourself a vino and I'll show you around.'

Giddy with excitement, he showed them up the stone staircase to the room underneath the turret. In the hearth, he'd lit a fire. And around an upturned tea-chest were arranged two wicker garden chairs and a tatty two-seater sofa. Maybe it was the wine, or perhaps just the fact that they were miles away from anywhere, but Jack's boss seemed younger somehow. And in the flickering glow of the flames, he began to see Mancini in a new light altogether. His skin was more olive – and his pomade drenched quiff more luscious. He'd even made a few concessions to his regulation 1950s garb. His trademark trilby hat and tie were gone. His sleeves were rolled up. And most shocking of all, he was wearing his braces down! While still a good 10 years older than the rest of them, tonight he seemed less like Jack's boss and more like a handsome older brother. And the warmth of his welcome was verging on motherly!

'Come on in, come on in,' he said, beckoning them into the only warm room in the tower and refilling their glasses. 'Saluti!'

But before George could enjoy his second glass, he caught his shoe in a dip in the uneven floor, fell back into the old sofa, and spilled the whole glass of red down his shirt, causing them all to disintegrate into a fit of giggles. Jack quickly saw an opportunity to tease his boyfriend once more.

'All right, Mr DeMille, I think Georgie boy is ready for his close-up!' he cried, before jumping on the sofa and picking up where he'd left off with the kiss in the Morris.

'Get off me! No! Don't you dare!' protested George, as Jack thrust his tongue into his mouth. But despite being damp – and a little bit embarrassed – he couldn't remember ever feeling quite so happy.

Chapter Ten

Make mine a Glemonade!

Monday 21st October 2019 – 9am – Zarathustra Advertising, New York

Arriving at Zarathustra Advertising, New York with a few minutes to spare, Cameron thought he'd use the time to have one last run through his pitch for Rakewell's Gin. Seeing there was a queue at reception, he headed for a seat cut into the 6ft letter 't' that formed part of the agency's name running the length of the ground-floor window. What passers-by thought of the mishmash of 20 and 30-somethings sitting in, on, or leaning against, the various letters of the agency's moniker, was anyone's guess. Though Cameron suspected that even some of the loungers and leaners themselves would be hard pushed to explain exactly what the agency actually did. Himself included. Even after reading the palm-sized booklet that had accompanied the recent merging of several agencies under this single name.

Apparently, according to the booklet, *Zarathustra* was a Persian priest-turned-prophet from way back when, who was quite a hit with the movers and shakers of the ancient world. This was, it seemed, where the similarity with the agency's namesake ended. While Zarathustra – the prophet – is credited with being first to wrestle with biggies like the notions of heaven and hell and judgement after death, Zarathustra – the advertising agency – was content to bother itself only with the future of its clients' marketing needs. The latest product innovation. The newest and most exciting media channel. The next emerging market. A bright shiny future, seen through the crystal ball of Zarathustra's marketing teams.

On the first reading of his *'brand in the hand'*, Cameron had been unable to reconcile the blurb in the booklet with the weighty questions to which Zarathustra – the prophet – had devoted his life. But after one particularly thorny client meeting Cameron had endured recently, he realised that the brand bods were on the right track after all. *Client management was absolute hell.*

Thankfully though, today wasn't about managing. The pitch presentation for the relaunch of Rakewell's Gin was about selling. Distilled in London since the 1960s, the gin brand was suffering from a bit of an image problem, and Zarathustra was one of the agencies invited to give it a bit of a refresh. Now part of a global drinks company based in the States, the new owner's strategy was to target the relaunch initially at the LGBTIQ+ community before broadening its appeal to a wider youth audience. *'Get the gays, and the kids will follow!'* as Donald Hunter, Rakewell's boorish CEO, was apt to say – whenever the opportunity arose. It was the reason Cameron suspected he had been asked to head up the pitch. Not just because he was gay, but also because of his work on a number of clothing and tech brands that had been successful at attracting the youth market. Though a working knowledge of 'the gays' and 'the kids' weren't the only weapons in Cameron's armoury. He also knew how to handle stubborn old goats like Hunter. Growing up on a sheep farm in Perthshire, it was par for the course. Just one of the many qualities that had propelled Cameron's upward trajectory in the business and landed him the role of group account director at Zarathustra London. *Aye, no bad for a poofter from Perthshire.* As Cameron was apt to say – whenever the opportunity arose.

Yet as he glanced around the room of millennials connected to their phones and laptops, he couldn't help feeling that he was increasingly disconnected from the industry to which he had devoted his life thus far. The cause of this malaise? Cameron wasn't entirely sure. The internet? Social media? Perhaps he was just getting a wee bit long in the tooth for an industry that these days preferred *big* data to *big* ideas. A world that seemed to fetishize anything that was considered innovative, shiny or new. Even if, in most cases, it was just the repackaging of something that was as old as the hills on his dad's farm.

In the last week, for instance, he'd not only been reliably informed by a heavily tattooed 'digital planner' that binding old bits of soap together to make one big bar was this week's number one trending 'life-hack'. But he'd also been enlightened by a young copywriter called Jade that 'the best stories have a beginning, middle and an end'. Resisting the urge to scream after hearing this particular life-changing insight had required from him the mastery of composure and calm he suspected the Buddha had experienced just before reaching Nirvana. How many more straws like these his camel's back could support, Cameron did not know. But the job was well paid. And smart-arse whippersnappers aside, it was not overly stressful. So, befitting someone working in an industry that had turned speaking in metaphors into an art-form, he decided to keep his powder dry, hold his horses, and resist the urge to throw in the towel. For a little while longer at least. Mid-life crisis averted, he reached into his satchel for his laptop and a last-minute run through his presentation.

Ping!

Too late. Hearing the lift and seeing a middle-aged blonde woman ice-picking her way over to him in stiletto heels, he told his face to smile and prepared himself for the onslaught. As he did so, a strange thought occurred to him. *Perhaps there were people here who could predict the future after all.* How else did they know he was in the building when he hadn't even signed in yet? More likely he had been spotted by some well-positioned account executive, briefed to look out for a skinny fella with shoulder-length red hair, wearing a tight-fitting suit; his trademark look that could easily have been gleaned from the company website. Whatever the source of his swift discovery, the moment to perform had arrived.

'Cameron!' hollered the blonde bombshell, still a good 10 yards away from him, but on target for a direct hit. *So, this was the force of nature that was Bunny Goldman, the woman who would be his US counterpart on the gin business – should his agency win it.*

'So great to meet in the flesh, finally. How *are* you? And how was your flight?' she gushed with the kind of enthusiasm Brits usually reserved for greeting long-lost friends. But where Bunny really excelled, Cameron soon discovered, was in her ability to make him feel like he was in cahoots with something both hugely important, but at the same time, faintly ridiculous. Shaking the hand of a middle-aged woman called Bunny – in the shadow of a six-foot letter 't' – certainly seemed to support this hypothesis.

'Aye, the flight wasn't bad, thanks for asking,' he replied politely, adroitly aware that most questions wrapped up in American greetings required no answer. Pleasantries over, Bunny spun around and began the return trip to the lift at almost the same speed as before.

'We're in Windsor. On the 6th. Thought it would dial up our British credentials,' she continued, her hand now firmly gripped around the metaphorical talking stick. 'I've already whizzed Donald and his minions through your ideas. He loves your strapline and the idea for experiential. *Make mine a Glemonade!* Thinks it's priceless. *I'll have a Glemonade, my old mucka!* he keeps saying in his godawful Britisher accent. If we can get the soda company on board, between you and me, I think it's in the bag. Everyone's really excited. *Keen as mustard*, as you lot say. Just need to sort out the numbers. All good. Great buzz.'

Over the course of the previous month, Cameron had got used to Bunny's machine-gun patter via the numerous conference calls about the pitch. *More like drive-by shootings than business meetings!* he'd once joked to Alex. Meeting her in person was an even greater assault on the senses. Though he was looking forward to seeing the corner of the agency that she promised would be forever England. Of course, these had not been her exact words. But the dartboard, framed Beatles photographs and bust of Churchill did go some way to explain her previous comment about the room. As did the suit of armour where Donald Hunter, of the '*gays and the kids*' comment, was holding court. Certainly, if shaking hands with a middle-aged woman called Bunny in front of a 6ft letter 't' had not quite proved his theory that he was involved in something faintly ridiculous, the few moments spent schmoozing Hunter in the shadow of King Arthur did the trick.

After a few minutes of small talk, Cameron's attention drifted over to a handsome young account executive attempting to connect his laptop to the AV. Pleased to be given an excuse to break free from Donald, he made his apologies and joined the laddie in front of the plasma screen at the other end of the room.

'Cheers, doll. I can take it from here... Er sorry, we've not been introduced.'

'Oh, hi. I'm Richard. But most people call me Dick.'

'Och! I definitely prefer Dick,' replied Cameron mischievously, making the boy's apple pie cheeks turn even rosier than they were already.

Oh, I suppose the job does have its perks, after all, he thought to himself as his gaze followed Dick's bubble butt to the other end of the table. And besides, the hard work had already been done. The look and feel had been captured on mood-boards. The typography had been graphically designed to within an inch of its kerning. Better looking agency folk had been commandeered to appear in rough versions of ads that would later be re-shot at huge expense by some fancy director and thrust into the social media feeds of thousands of trendsetters and influencers. Copy had been painstakingly written, re-written and then returned to its original version. And budgets and costings, often the most creative bit of any pitch, had been copied from some previous job and massaged into reassuringly dull-looking charts and spreadsheets. Now all he had to do was convince the client that his agency could make *'the gays and the kids'* think Rakewell's Gin was cool again.

Cameron. Lies. Action.

'Rakewell's Gin. The gin that made the 60s swing!'

Chapter Eleven

Bewitched and bewildered

Wednesday 23rd October 2019 – 6pm – Bear Road, Brighton

'Et tu, Brute?' announced Izzy, popping her head around the lounge door in a Roman soldier helmet and brandishing a butter knife. Ken had been right; the trunk in their attic had indeed contained a costume he could wear to the upcoming Winter Tableaux Vivants. In addition, what she'd discovered amongst his aunt's belongings had done wonders to lift her mood since the humiliation of her poorly attended post-funeral gathering. On the day, she'd barely been able to contain her anger as she handed out vol-au-vents and platitudes to the sorry huddle of B-list guests who had turned up to watch the cortège from her lounge window; the filler crowd of neighbours invited merely to pad out the really interesting people from her new social circle, who, aside from Maria and Meena, had failed to materialise. But with every new find in the attic, thoughts of how she would punish the no-shows gradually dissipated, and by Wednesday evening, she'd licked her wounds and was ready for battle once again. Albeit with a butter knife.

'I think Brutus is supposed to do the stabbing, darling,' said Ken, over the top of his newspaper.

'Oh yes. Good point,' replied Izzy, removing the leather helmet and making herself comfortable on the sofa. 'And you were right about Paula's stash too. Though it's not just Roman costumes. There's loads of stuff. Police uniforms. Military gear. Cowboy outfits. There's even a feather headdress!'

'Oh my God. Do you think she had the Village People up there?' said Ken, dramatically crunching down his paper defences.

Ignoring her husband's quip, Izzy continued unperturbed.

'There's a whole box of theatrical backdrops as well. A real Aladdin's cave.'

'That's Paula the Hoarder!' said Ken, disappearing behind his newspaper again.

'And best of all. I found this!'

'Ugh!' sighed Ken, peering over his paper wall.

'I wonder what could be on it?' she said, proudly nestling a shallow metal tin about the size of a side-plate – of the sort designed to hold a reel of film. 'Says 'Yanks are Coming' on the side. I've looked it up online and there's a couple of films with the same title. One dating from 1942 and another from the early 70s.'

'Oooh, now that *is* interesting,' said Ken, folding up his paper and shoving it down the side of the armchair. 'Before she came back to Brighton, Paula did work in the film industry. Spent some time at British MGM in Borehamwood in the late 60s, I think. Even worked on *2001: A Space Odyssey.*'

'Oh, wow! Proper cult stuff! The ones I found online look more like war films. Exciting though, isn't it? And who knows? The reel inside might have nothing to do with the tin at all.'

As a curator at Brighton Museum, the prospect of discovering a family heirloom in her attic had Izzy's heart racing.

'Just imagine, Ken…'

'What I can imagine, darling, is you spending the next few weeks holed up in the attic sifting through Paula's hoard with a fine-toothed comb. Oh, how the winter months are going to fly by!' said Ken cutting across her and reaching for his paper.

'Well, you never know, darling. I have a meeting at Hove Museum in a couple of weeks. I'll see if they've got an old projector I can.…' she continued. But before she could finish, she was stopped mid-sentence once again. Not this time by her husband, but by the loud haha-haha cackle of a seagull somewhere nearby. And judging from the look that Ken gave her, he'd heard it too.

'Well, you be careful, love. You don't want to wake any ghosts. Paula wasn't someone who took kindly to being woken up when she was alive, so I don't rate your chances now she's dead.'

'Oh, stop it!' she said, brushing aside his allusion to Paula being reincarnated in the guise of a pesky seagull.

'Just getting you into the Hallowe'en spirit, cariña.'

There was a pause.

'Actually. Funny you should say that because…'

'Oh God no. Not another gath… ahem… another party?'

'Yes, dear,' said Izzy, noting – and ignoring – her husband's slip.

'I'm pretty sure no one's doing anything for Hallowe'en this year. And I've found the perfect outfit for you in Paula's hoard.'

'Well, I know the Village People were quite scary but…'

'No, darling. A shirt with ruffled collars and sleeves and a long military tunic. Slick your hair back and paint your face white and you'd be a dead ringer for Nosferatu! Especially with those ears!' she said, giggling to herself.

'I'll ring around tonight and get everyone geed up.' Keen to avoid a second social flop, she knew that inviting guests by phone would put them on the spot and leave no room for argument.

'Mmmm,' said Ken, unfolding his newspaper.

But before the geeing up could commence, her mobile started ringing.

It was her sister Maria.

'Ah. Buenos tardes,' said Izzy.

'Buenos tardes, cariña. Que tal?

'Muy bien,' gushed Izzy, unable to contain her excitement. 'In fact, I was just about to call you. I've made the most wonderful discovery – '

'Oh my goodness, you've heard already!'

It was clear to Izzy that they were not talking about the same thing. A chest of fancy-dress costumes and props that belonged to Ken's Aunt Paula was unlikely the cause of Maria's excitement. Izzy decided to play it cool. Perhaps she could work it out for herself.

'I could hardly believe it when Adam told us this morning. Imagine! Our new home mentioned in a gay love letter from the 1960s. Increible!'

What was 'increible' was that twice in as many weeks, something had happened that had completely passed Izzy by. First Grace's death, and now this! Was she losing her touch? She decided to hold her nerve a little longer and see what Maria might give away.

'Especially as one of the lovers is so well known. Well, in Brighton anyway. Who'd have thought it, Bette Y'Sweet Ass and his lover, meeting up at Coleshill all those years ago!'

Izzy's plan seemed to be working. Clearly a letter had turned up that suggested Maria and Meena's new home had once been the venue for some gay assignation.

'And if they hadn't needed to use those old hymn books at the funeral – Cameron would never have found it.'

Un-fucking-believable. Of all the people in Brighton whose hands it could have fallen into. Cameron-fucking-MacIntyre. Despite her irritation, Izzy kept her expletives to herself and let Maria continue.

'It all makes sense now, doesn't it? The old man at the farm, mistaking me for some *chico* who used to live at the abbey. I mentioned it at yours last week. Remember?'

'Well, you do look quite boyish, cariña,' laughed Izzy, referring to Maria's crew cut.

'Si… supongo… I suppose so. Although the old man's daughter did say his memory wasn't what it used to be.'

'Ha. Mine neither. Remind me, cariña. What were they doing at the abbey all those years ago?' enquired Izzy, cleverly using Maria's last comment to her advantage.

'No one knows. Cameron has given Ollie the job of finding out. Apparently, Bette is his neighbour. He's going to see what he can find out this week.'

This week? Good. There was still time to steal some of Cameron's thunder. Hallowe'en at hers would take the focus away from his recent discovery. Hopefully by then, Ollie would have had chance to talk to Bette. And hosting the occasion for his big reveal would be the perfect way to get back in the game. So, with memories of the post-funeral gathering put to bed, Izzy ended her call with her sister and searched for the number of the guest of honour. Oliver Simpson.

Chapter Twelve

Whose tag-line is it anyway?

Thursday 24th October 2019 – 10am – Zarathustra Advertising, London

The day after Cameron returned to the UK, the New York office called to say his team had won the pitch for Rakewell's Gin. As such, his first job on Thursday was to fire off a 'thank you' email to anyone in the agency who'd been involved. No matter how scant their contribution. No matter how insignificant their role. In fact, in recent times this had meant thanking the mailroom for delivering parcels, receptionists for being welcoming, and kitchen staff for making lime green cup-cakes in honour of a prospective client's rather lurid branding. In other words, thanking people for doing the job for which they were paid. 'Thank you' email, sent, Cameron made his way to the boardroom to meet the people who had genuinely been part of the pitch-winning team. There before him already was the copywriter who had come up with the line about Rakewell's Gin making the 60s swing.

'Well done, Thomas laddie,' said Cameron, as he entered the room.

'Thanks, mate,' replied the young man, in a public-school accent – somewhat incongruous with his Hell's Angel attire. 'Well done to you, too!'

How refreshing, thought Cameron, fully aware that recognising the contribution made by anyone other than themselves was a rare thing amongst Creatives – who generally believed that ideas sold themselves.

Mutual appreciation over, the approaching hubbub in the corridor outside announced the arrival of the rest of the team. First through the door was Emma, the art-buyer. A deceptive title since, as far as Cameron was aware, her job never required buying any actual art. Rather her remit was liaising with the designers, photographers and illustrators, who were often integral to the ad campaigns that agencies pumped out. Next up was head of traffic, Rhoda. Again, misleading. *Had she ever shepherded cars through the streets of London?* Cameron thought not. What he did know, however, was that her job was a 'thankless task'. Everyone said so. Most notably Rhoda herself. Though given the enormous sway her department held over the working lives of agency folk – deciding when and to whom jobs were briefed – Cameron was certain Rhoda and her team received more thanks for their toil than most. After Rhoda and Emma came a couple of 'suits' – agency slang for those whose job it was to sell the creative work. Harking back to the dress-code of advertising executives from a bygone age, this again was a bit of a misnomer. The truth was that aside from board-members like Cameron, who still saw themselves as latter-day Madmen, hardly anyone at Zarathustra – or any other agency for that matter – wore a suit anymore. Case in point was senior account director, Katlyn – dressed in combats and T-shirt – who handled the day-to-day running of the agency's booze portfolio. And just behind her – in chinos and rugby shirt – an account supervisor called Greg; a chap who was so classically good-looking he was known to everyone as

'Handsome Greg'. A nickname that Cameron thought was a wee bit unfair on the other two Gregs at the agency. Last to enter the board room was art director, Rob, the other half of the creative team on Rakewell's Gin, wearing – ironically enough – a suit.

'OK,' said Cameron, signalling that the meeting was about to start. 'As you know, I presented the work to the client in New York on Monday, and by and large, it was well received. Since then, I've had an email from Bunny with some more feedback and a clear direction of how they want us to proceed.' *Ah, no giggling for a change.* Much like how the mention of anal warts no longer raises a smile from people who work at a clap clinic, it appeared that his team had finally got used to the concept of a middle-aged woman answering to the name of Bunny. But before Cameron could get on with the feedback, Rhoda had a question.

'And they still want to go live in January, yes?'

'Yes, Rhoda. Still January.' Cameron knew she knew it was January. Rhoda had just scored 1 point in the popular advertising agency game known as Bullshit Bingo – in which colleagues show each other how important and clever they are.

'That means we'll need to have our *influencer strategy* in place by mid-December if we want to *piggy-back* on LGBT History Month,' piped in Katlyn, dropping in not one, but two buzzwords and earning herself 2 points.

'Thank you, Katlyn,' said Cameron. 'You raise a good point, too. The client likes the idea of hooking up with a lemonade brand, but the concept for experiential—'

'Oh, here we go,' interrupted Rob, giving away the probable truth that *'Make mine a Glemonade!'* had been *his* idea.

'And what about the tag-line?' chirped in Thomas.

'Oh. They absolutely love *'The gin that made the 60s swing'*. That's definitely going ahead,' said Cameron. 'What they're not so keen on though are the celebs we suggested to front the relaunch. The ones they do like, they can't afford. The others, they think are a bit too safe.'

'So, we need to come up with a *brand ambassador* who is cool… but also cheap,' summarised Thomas, earning him a point for brand ambassador.

'Aye, that's about the long and the short of it,' conceded Cameron. 'But the joint venture with a lemonade company is definitely on the table still. So, all in all, I think we're in a really good place.'

Known in the business as a 'shit sandwich', Cameron had expertly slotted the bad news inside two bits of good and earned himself 3 Bullshit Bingo points in the process. So, final scores on the doors. Katlyn 2 points. Thomas and Rhoda, one point each. Rob and Greg, zero. And the winner – the biggest bullshitter of them all – Cameron, on 3. Game – and meeting – over, an agreement was made to regroup the following week and one by one they all left the room until Cameron was on his own.

He glanced at his phone to check the time and catch up on the messages he'd received in the last hour. Most interesting of these was a text from Alex with a link to the Egyptian mummy costume he wanted Cameron to order for Izzy's Hallowe'en party. *Poor Izzy.* She'd had her nose well and truly put out of joint with the poorly attended post-funeral gathering. It wouldn't hurt him to cut her a little slack. Allow her this little fancy-dress party at least. Especially as he'd already picked out a rather dashing Dracula costume to wear for himself. With that in mind, he tapped on his calendar to set a reminder to collect his and

Alex's outfits. But on doing so, another idea suddenly entered his head instead.

'Perfect!' he said out loud to the now empty room.

To his delight, he noticed that the weekend after Izzy's party would be the ideal one to celebrate Bonfire Night. No one, to his knowledge, had arranged anything for that date yet, so it would be the ideal way to maintain his position at the centre of his social circle. He tapped into Facebook Messenger and sent an invite to 30 of his closest friends.

BONFIRE BONANZA! Saturday 2nd November.
Join us for an evening of fireworks, food and fizz.
Fun and flames start at 7pm.

With the same satisfaction a medieval she-wolf might feel when signing a death warrant, Cameron had effectively snuffed out any talk of Izzy's upcoming Hallowe'en party. The focus of conversation would now move to his Bonfire Bonanza instead! While his mobile replaced the parchment, and his cold coffee, a goblet of wine, the malicious intent was the same. *Don't want you getting ideas above your station, do we, lassie!* Sabotage complete, he gathered his things and left.

Chapter Thirteen

Tell me where the pane is

**Saturday 26th October 2019 – 6am –
Ditchling Rise Studios, Preston Park**

The buzz of an alarm at 6am on a Saturday morning was not a noise with which Ollie was especially familiar. The sound of Dora Bryan lurching up the hill outside his flat, however, was something he recognised immediately. Although, in fairness, he knew it could just as easily have been Aubrey Beardsley, Dusty Springfield or Virginia Woolf. Or any of the other celebrities with connections to the city after whom the local bus fleet were named. But Ollie had a soft spot for old Dora, so he decided it was her. He opened one eye and looked down at the arm wrapped around his waist. On the bicep, he could clearly see a tattoo of a cherub. Narrowing his eyes to extend his vision a little further, he could just about make out the feathery clouds on which the chubby babe was seated. And completing the scene were the rays of sunshine in which both cloud and angel were bathed. The sun itself, being drawn high on Drew's shoulder blade, was inconveniently out of view. Woken, but not quite awake, Ollie wallowed in his half-sleep for a few moments. *Two weeks and five days!* An anniversary of sorts. Not *quite* a record, but not far off! And since meeting they had seen each other almost every day – and most nights too. It was no surprise then that Ollie had become rather familiar with the artwork wrapped around Drew's muscular frame. And the canvas on which it was drawn. But the attraction went way beyond his gorgeous body. The Welshman was incredible in the sack. Great down the pub. And most importantly of all; he'd got the seal of approval from Ollie's friends. Or to be more precise – he'd survived their prodding and probing. *And what a face!*

Wriggling free from the embrace, Ollie turned to the handsome head resting on his pillow. Cutesy pug nose. Plump rosy lips. And though the lids were closed, he knew that beneath them were the most gorgeous blue eyes. *Woof!* He thought to himself. Or had he, in fact, said it out loud? Whichever it was, Drew's eyelids suddenly scrunched open to reveal two spheres of brilliant sapphire. Ollie's heart skipped a beat.

'Bore da, babe,' yawned Drew, lifting his head and reaching for his phone on the bedside table, the source of the buzzing.

'Morning,' said Ollie with a smile, recognising one of the few words he knew in his boyfriend's native tongue.

'Just gone six actually,' said Drew, turning off his alarm.

'Best get a wiggle on then, if we're gonna get to your place before seven.'

'Oh shit. Your treasure-hunt!'

After George had revealed that the Duke's mentioned in the letter was not the Duke of York's cinema, but Duke's Garage – now Ditchling Rise Studios – where Drew ran his motor repair business, Ollie had done a bit of digging around online. Intrigued by some photos he'd found of the building in the 1930s – when it boasted beautiful art deco stained-glass windows bearing the garage's former name – he was keen to see it for himself. But after Drew mentioned an old desk that he'd found in the mechanics pit when he'd first moved into his unit a few years back, Ollie's request had a new urgency. According to Ollie's research, the garage had been derelict for decades before being remodelled in the mid-noughties. Remembering from his interview with George that the fella organising the trip to the old abbey was not only Jack's boss but also the owner of the garage back then, Ollie was curious to see if there might be something in the desk that would shed light on what George and his friends were doing at Coleshill all those years ago. He knew it was a long shot. *But stranger things had happened, hadn't they?* Like an old love letter turning up in an even older hymn book! *Surely it was worth a punt.* And with Izzy's Hallowe'en party later that day, Ollie was keen to see what he could find before he reported back about his interview with George. Even if it meant less time in bed with his handsome mechanic.

So, a quick shower and a motorbike ride later, they were outside the old building and ready to explore. Removing his helmet, Ollie noticed a solitary seagull on the stone arch that ran above the entrance. But other than the bird, it seemed that they had the place to themselves. A fact that made the visit even more thrilling for Ollie. Once inside, the next job was finding the old desk.

As beautiful as Drew remembered it being, with most of his documents and files stored on his computer, he'd had little use – and even less room – for the cumbersome antique, so had moved it out of the way until he could decide what to do with it. That had been five years ago. Since then it had remained in limbo in the cavernous storeroom which ran the length of the building's top floor.

'This is mad,' said Drew, undoing the door to the rarely entered chamber.

Ping, hmmmmm, ping, hummmm, ping…

Greeted by a series of fluorescent tubes firing up around them, Ollie suddenly found himself in a Tutankhamun-like tomb of crap.

'Jesus! What the…' gasped Ollie, gazing upon the rows and rows of discarded boxes and broken furniture that filled the space from floor to ceiling. Old desk-fans, rusty metal filing cabinets, bulky VDUs. There was even what looked like an industrial loom lurking in the shadows at the far end of the storeroom. Although given the age of some of the stuff piled up around him, he wouldn't have been surprised if it had been Alan Turing's code-breaker machine.

'Over here!' barked Drew, standing a few yards from where they had come in. 'Look at the fucker. I can't believe we carried it up all those stairs.'

'Yeah, I wish I'd known you back then. You must have been quite buff,' replied Ollie, spurned a little by the mention of Drew's ex; one half of the 'we' who had helped carry the desk upstairs.

'Fuck you, Twinkle Toes,' said Drew, studying the hulk of furniture. 'Oh bugger. It's back to front. We're gonna have to move it away from the wall.'

'OK. As long as you don't tread on my *twinkle toes*!' joked Ollie, joining Drew at one end of the desk.

In fact, had the wall actually been a wall, this plan would have worked just fine. But following one final joint effort, Drew pulling and Ollie pushing, all of a sudden there was an almighty crack. As they stopped to take a closer look, the reason soon became clear. Quite literally. What they had assumed was a wall, on closer inspection, turned out to be a window; painted over in thick black paint. More than that even. A little rubbing soon revealed it to be the stained-glass that bore the original name of the garage.

'Wow. The light up here must have been stunning back in the day,' said Ollie, pointing to the skylights that had also been blacked out.

'Yeah. It's criminal what little respect people have,' said Drew, shaking his head.

'I know! Like can you believe someone just dumped this desk up here?'

'Ha ha. Very funny. It's not like we covered the fucker in black paint is it!'

Feeling another twinge of jealousy at the mention of the ex-boyfriend, Ollie was keen to change the subject.

'So, how about we start rifling through your drawers?'

'Rifle away,' sniggered Drew.

Fired up by the possibility of finding some new clue to what George and his friends were doing at Coleshill all those years ago, before long, the contents of the bureau were piled high around them both. Bills. Newspapers. Boxes of dried cigarettes. Cigarette cards. Invoices. Old car mags. A girlie calendar. Car manuals. MOT certificates. Tax discs. Parking fines. Sweet wrappers. Crisp packets. A beautiful copper hip flask with a residue of whisky still inside it. Just a selection of what they found. Yet despite the significant haul – some of it indeed dating back to the 60s – it became increasingly likely that there was nothing in the bureau belonging to either George or Jack. Perhaps it had all gone up in smoke after all, thought Ollie, remembering what George had said the other evening about the fire at the old abbey. In fact, by the time he'd emptied the final drawer on the floor, the schoolboy excitement of hunting for treasure had all but left him, and the conversation turned instead to the Dr Jekyll and Mr Hyde costumes they had hired for the party later.

Until…

'Hang on a minute. What's this?'

Ollie turned to see Drew in a pose that reminded him of an old film he'd watched as a kid, called *It Shouldn't Happen to a Vet*. He couldn't remember the plot, but he seemed to recall that one of the things that most definitely *did* happen to a vet was that they would find themselves with their arm up a cow's arse at least once a week.

'What *are* you doing?' enquired Ollie.

'Gotcha!' replied Drew, pulling an envelope from the back of the drawer.

'Open it. Open it!' cried Ollie, his schoolboy excitement suddenly making a surprise come-back. As he tore back the envelope, seconds later a bundle of faded magazines spilled onto the concrete floor between them.

'Oh my God. It's porn!' cried Ollie with glee.

'Better than that, boyo,' began Drew, picking up a magazine called CHAMPION, which featured a youth in yellow and white striped trunks, gingerly gripping a large orange beach ball. 'It's fucking *gay* porn! Though whatever he's a champion of, it's certainly not volley-ball!' he added, pointing at the boy's camp pose.

Ollie, meanwhile, had been drawn to a magazine called *RAGAZZO*, featuring a youth in a posing pouch leaning over a stool like a latter-day *Thinker*, only with a 1960s bouffant quiff.

'Look!' said Ollie, pointing to a caption under the title. 'This one is the companion to another magazine called *UOMO*.'

'Ha. Good to see the daddy – twink relationship was already going strong back then,' sniggered Drew, putting *CHAMPION* to one side and picking up the final magazine in the *un*holy trinity.

'*Adonis Body – Studies in the Male Physique*,' he read out aloud before turning to the centre spread. 'Look! It's

Brad. By candlelight!' he cried, barely able to get the words out – he was laughing so much.

'At least he's found a comfortable spot to read his book,' added Ollie, feasting his eyes on a sulky looking teen who was reclining face down on a chaise-longue, his back and naked buttocks bathed in the light of a candelabra.

'Even though he seems to have lost his underwear in the process!' howled Drew, briefly regaining the power of speech before rolling on the floor in a fit of hysterics again.

'Aw. Quite sweet really,' said Ollie, once the sniggers had subsided.

'Hot too,' added Drew, flicking through *Adonis Body* and inhaling the musty smell of the paper as he did so. 'Why do all porn mags smell the same?'

'Mmmmm. I can think of one reason!'

Sprawled on the storeroom floor, flicking through mildewed soft porn mags from the 60s felt oddly nostalgic to Ollie. Swap *Adonis Body* and *RAGAZZO* for *Boys Own* and the *Beano* and he could have been with his first schoolboy crush, whiling away a wet afternoon at home in Birmingham. Until… suddenly it struck him.

'Oh my giddy aunt!' he exclaimed, breaking the quiet camaraderie.

'That cover! I've seen it before. In George's hallway. It's *him*. It's George. As a teenager!'

'Holy fuck! Are you sure?'

'Absolutely certain. I knew I recognised those eyes from somewhere! Oh my God! That's what they were doing at the abbey,' cried Ollie, pointing at the cover of *CHAMPION*.

'Shooting gay porn!'

Chapter Fourteen

The Ghostess with the Mostest

What with the feverish disembowelling of pumpkins – and an equally furious emptying of the attic – by the day of the Hallowe'en party, thoughts of her disastrous 'post-funeral gathering' had faded from Isobel Pitt's memory entirely, and she was in buoyant mood once again. As she suspected, the military cloak and the frilly shirt made a striking vampire outfit for Ken. And with a bit of padding, she'd also managed to transform the white cotton sheets she'd discovered at the bottom of Paula's trunk into a Victorian-style wedding dress. Complete with bustle and veil, once it had been sprayed with fake cobwebs, she had great expectations for her Miss Havisham inspired costume. Trying it on in front of the bedroom mirror, Izzy was especially thrilled with her baboon-sized posterior.

'Bottomless Pitt!' she said out loud, recalling the nickname she heard that Cameron had come up with to make fun of her lithe figure. 'Not tonight, I won't be!'

'What's that?' said Josh, looking up from his phone for a moment; his presence, another reason for her good mood. As Ken had predicted, the novelty of doing his own laundry *had* worn off after a few days, and their Prodigal Son had moved back in shortly before the ill-fated post-funeral gathering.

'Bottomless Pitt, darling. Apparently, it's what the Velociraptors are calling me behind my back,' replied Izzy, referring to what she called Cameron, Alex and Adam, behind theirs.

'OMG. That's hilarious!' laughed Josh, from the dressing-table chair on which he had plonked his own bottom. 'Which one of the dinosaurs came up with that one?'

'Who do you think?'

'I thought so. Bit pot-kettle don't you think of Mr Skinny Pants? Still, he's quite hot for an old fella.'

Izzy stopped playing with her bustle and shot him a look of horror.

'If you're into that sort of thing,' he added, more sheepishly. 'Which I'm not... BTW.'

Clearly, her white powdered complexion and heavily blacked-up eyes were more chilling than she had realised. But the sentiment was real enough. She had only just got used to her son liking boys. She hadn't considered that he might also be into men! Relieved by his assurances that he had no 'daddy' issues, Izzy decided to let it pass and returned to safer ground.

'You and Kwan are more than welcome to join us tonight, you know,' she said, referring to the 'age-appropriate' boyfriend with whom Josh had temporarily shared a washing machine recently.

'Ha. No thanks. A bunch of pensioners high on weed – *and God knows what else* – prancing around in face-paint and fancy-dress! I'd rather stick pins in my eyes,' he replied.

Phew, thought Izzy. Despite Josh's admiration for Cameron's Wildean wit, it seemed that a joke at her expense was all he wanted to share with her nemesis.

'We're watching *28 Days Later*. That'll be enough *zombie creeping flesh* for one night, I think. No need to experience the real thing!'

She gasped at his insult. Though in truth, she was impressed with his bitchy bon mot. He may have got his looks from Ken, but Izzy was certain that Josh's penchant for acerbic repartee had been learnt at his mother's knee.

'OK, I'm off,' he announced suddenly, leaping out of the chair and striding towards the bedroom door. Pausing momentarily on the landing, he turned for a second and gave her a once over. 'Costume looks great, Mum. You'll be the Ghostess with the Mostest!' And with that, he was gone.

'Ghostess with the Mostest,' she repeated to herself, as she heard the front door slam and his footsteps gradually disappear down the hill. And while she knew that, strictly speaking, Miss Havisham wasn't a ghost, she loved the sound of it and made a mental note to pass it off as her own later on. She was equally thrilled with the theatrical backdrops she'd discovered in the attic. Pinned to the walls and festooned in more of those fake cobwebs, they gave the downstairs rooms a fabulous nightmarish quality. Palatine Hills of Ancient Rome in the lounge. A Wild West scene in the hall. The turrets and onion domes of an Arabian cityscape in the kitchen. And once the pumpkin lanterns had been lit and placed on the front steps, the Ghostess with the Mostest was ready to take centre stage. *Who cared if Cameron was planning something for Bonfire Night?* No one would be up for another fancy-dress party so soon after tonight. And there's no way he could compete with the treasures of Paula's hoard. She glanced at her watch to check the time. The witching hour – or 7.30 for 8, as she had said in the invite – had arrived. And minutes later, so did her guests.

First through the door were Maria and Meena – the former dressed as Little Miss Muffet and the latter as an eight-legged spider. Thrown by the sight of her sister with long hair and a skirt – a look she hadn't seen Maria sporting since they were girls in Spain – Izzy instinctively fell into her native tongue.

'Ah, mis amores. Tan precioso. Me encantan tus disfraces!'

'Gracias, Señorita Havisham. I love your costume too,' replied Meena, from behind the hairy spider mask. Usually the more feminine of the pair – preferring to wear her silvery grey hair long and rarely seen without lipstick – Meena's transformation was equally spooky.

'And Ken! Nosferatu is it? Que guapo!' squealed Maria.

'Thank you, Miss Muffet! Let me find you a tuffet. And Mr Spider, perhaps somewhere to sit beside her!' said Ken, in his attempt at a Transylvanian accent.

Next up the steps was Stephen – as the Wicked Witch of the East. Though it quickly transpired that the animal he'd brought with him on his broom that evening was more canine than the feline.

'I'm so sorry, Izzy. My sitter let me down at the last minute, and I couldn't leave Mr Ben on his own this close to Bonfire Night,' apologised Stephen from under his pointy hat as he dragged the hound over the threshold and gave him a dog-chew. Wincing slightly from the mention of Bonfire Night – Cameron's Facebook invite still fresh in her mind – Izzy forced a smile and made some comment about how she thought fireworks should be banned. Stephen responded with a gushing appraisal of Izzy's costume and placated by the compliment, the Ghostess with the Mostest returned to the task of handing out chunks of chorizo and fielding questions from her invited guests.

Yes, we found the backdrops in the attic. No, I haven't heard anything more about the letter. Yes, Ollie was definitely coming. No, I don't have any crème de menthe!

In fact, Izzy was so busy playing the Ghostess with the Mostest, she missed the arrival of Cameron and his fellow Velociraptors, Adam and Alex. Disappointing mainly because when she did finally spot them, it appeared that Cameron had committed the most cardinal of fancy-dress sins by turning up in the same costume – more or less – as his host. *How he must have squirmed being greeted by Ken dressed as Nosferatu – a far classier version of the Hallowe'en favourite.* Accompanied by Adam, as a horny little devil – and Alex, as a mummy – Izzy made her way over to the trio for a closer inspection.

'Good evening, gentleman, what are you all gassing about?' she asked, brandishing a plate of skewered garlic prawns. As she suspected they were discussing the letter. 'Oh, I know all about that. I want news, *not* history, darling!'

'History is the *news,* darling!' shrieked the mummy. At least that's what she thought he said because the bandages wrapped around Alex's head made him difficult to understand. But without an update from Ollie, there would be neither news nor history. *What could be keeping him?* She'd set her heart on his interview with the old drag queen being the centrepiece of the party. But since he had yet to turn up, the conversation moved naturally onto other upcoming events. Most thrilling of all, Maria and Meena's Tableaux Vivants; made all the more exciting by the fact that their new home was the likely venue for some mysterious gathering mentioned in the infamous letter.

Working the room with platefuls of tapas, Izzy learnt that Stephen – and Mr Ben – would be regaling them all as Sir Lancelot and Queen Guinevere. Though it wasn't certain who would be who. Adam and his 'yet to be confirmed' plus one would be Narcissus and his reflection. Even more appropriate than his devil outfit, thought Izzy. And as for the hostesses; Meena was currently in the middle of making an enormous scallop shell for her role as Venus, and Maria – as Sappho – was going to be doing something with a big quill. But after a while, even the stream of chatter about the Tableaux Vivants began to run dry. Thankfully, just as Izzy feared the conversation would turn to Cameron's hastily organised Bonfire Bonanza, she spied the guest of honour and his new boyfriend in top hats and lamb-chop sideburns. Lit by the glow of pumpkin lanterns as they skipped up the steps to the front door, she immediately recognised them as the tragic pair from Robert Louis Stevenson's gothic novella; even though Ollie's cheeky grin made for the least evil Mr Hyde she'd ever seen, and certainly there were few doctors as cute as Jekyll down at her local surgery. Handing a plate of albondigas to Ken, she rushed to the front door to greet them. After all the effort she had made, Izzy was determined that any glory from what Ollie had discovered would be reflected on her – not on Cameron. It was *her* party. They were *her* guests. It would be *her* glory. Welcoming them into the house as if they had been returning war heroes, she quickly ushered Ollie and Drew into the lounge where the other guests were waiting for the update. Pleasantries exchanged and glasses charged, Izzy decided it was time for the main event. So, with an *oh so casual* mention of an upcoming exhibition at the museum about local queer history – moments later, Ollie was regaling them all with what he had found out from Bette.

And so much more besides.

'Yes. Jack was George's lover! A car crash... I know, tragic... Mancini was Jack's boss... and Paula... a friend who worked at the Theatre Royal... meeting at Coleshill, yes... no, not Duke of York's cinema... Duke's Garage... the building where Drew now works... old desk... gay porn!'

'Gay porn!' shrieked Izzy, on hearing about the magazines that the boys had discovered at the old garage.

'Well, what counted as gay porn back then,' said Ollie, handing Izzy the copy of *RAGAZZO* and giving *Adonis Body* to Cameron.

'Bodybuilding and a bit of dressing up really.'

'Dressing up?' enquired Meena from the floor, unable to find a tuffet big enough to accommodate all of her eight spider legs.

'Greek gods, Roman soldiers... that sort of thing.'

Roman soldiers? How odd, thought Izzy, catching Ken's eye over the top of *RAGAZZO*.

'Mainly young men in posing pouches and swimming costumes,' continued Ollie. 'Pretty tame by today's standards.'

'It's no Grindr that's for sure,' quipped Cameron, showing Adam a spread featuring a youngster in a boxing pose.

'Phwaooor!' was his predictable response.

'Do you think? Bit too butch for me,' laughed Cameron.

'Bitch!' cried Alex, rather confirming his husband's previous point.

'Aye well, it certainly has a whiff of the past about it,' Cameron said, sniffing the centre spread of his yellowing mag before passing it on to Adam and Alex. 'But what makes you think it's what they were doing at the abbey?'

Expecting this very question, Ollie had held back the copy of *CHAMPION* for the big reveal.

'Because of this!' he announced, holding the magazine in both hands for all to see. 'It's George! He has the same picture in his hallway.'

'No. Are you sure?' said Izzy.

'I'm absolutely certain. I knew there was something familiar about it when I was there last. Show them the pics, Drew,' said Ollie, excitedly. Half expecting that his friends would need more convincing, the boys had found some photos online of Bette from the early 80s.

'Feck, I think you're right!' roared Adam, clasping his head in disbelief and knocking his devil horns to the floor. Passing the magazine and phone around, one by one, they all agreed that the boy on the front cover had to be George.

'And what about this Jack fella? Which one's he?' enthused Cameron.

'I don't know. George has been away the last few days. He doesn't know about the magazines we found at Drew's garage yet.'

The ghosts, ghouls and blood-sucking vampires that Izzy now called friends were absolutely gripped. Passion. Drama. Death. And it was all happening in her front lounge. *That's one in the eye for MacIntyre,* she thought to herself. But there was one question still hanging in the air. The mention of Roman costumes… the talk of photo shoots and cameras… some woman called Paula. It was too much of a coincidence, surely? She suspected from the look he'd given her earlier that Ken was thinking the same. Of course, as an academic, she'd dismissed the thought that Paula's soul was being channelled by an inquisitive seagull. But that Ken had been thinking a lot about his aunt since they had begun sorting through her stuff in the attic, she was absolutely certain. An observation confirmed moments later when, signalling that he was about to speak, he loudly cleared his throat.

'And Paula? The woman who worked at the Theatre Royal. What did George say about her?'

'Oh yes,' said Ollie. 'Not much I'm afraid. He said he'd heard she'd passed away a couple of years ago.'

'Yes, I think he's right,' began Ken, his tone gradually silencing the group of friends. '18 months to be precise.'

He paused and took a gulp of wine.

'The thing is… I'm pretty certain that… that Paula is my aunt.'

'The one who left us all this…' added Izzy, waving her hands at the theatrical backdrops pinned to the walls. 'And…' Knowing the drama that was about to be released, she stopped mid-sentence for a few seconds before delivering the punchline.

'A reel of film!'

The effect was immediate. But in between the gasps and expletives, there was one person's reaction that Izzy was most keen to savour. Whether the colour had drained from Cameron's face at that precise moment, she could not tell – caked as it was in vampire white panstick. But the look of horror in his eyes – no doubt triggered by the news that Izzy was in possession of something that could potentially trump his letter. That was proving more difficult for him to hide. Barely able to disguise her joy at unexpectedly gaining the upper hand, Izzy thought the evening couldn't get any better. Until…

'Benito! Nooooooo!'

Turning towards the source of the commotion, the unfolding scene could hardly have pleased her more. Having picked up the scent of rubber in Adam's devil horns, Mr Ben had lost interest in his chew and climbed onto the arm of a chair to get a closer look at his new desire. Unable to reach the prize, he had instead grabbed a loose bandage dangling from Alex's wrist and was at that precise moment unravelling the whole outfit.

Oh God. I love that dog! Izzy smiled to herself.

Chapter Fifteen

More front than Brighton!

Saturday 26th October 2019 – evening – Brighton Pier

What with the wake, the funeral and meetings with lawyers about Grace's estate, George had barely had a minute to himself since his friend's passing. So, his trip to Monza, a small village just outside Milan where Grace had requested her ashes be scattered, had provided a much-needed break. It was also the first chance he'd had to properly say goodbye. How thoughtful of her to choose such a pleasant part of the world, thought George, on hearing her request in the will; one of several additions she'd made to the wish-list she'd written with him all those years before. And how fortunate she chose to go at this time of the year when it was still warm enough to sit outside and enjoy a little of *la dolce vita* before winter set in good and proper.

But he was happy to be back home. In fact, he'd missed the old place so much he felt the urge to take a stroll on the pier. Ordinarily it would be teeming with tourists on a Saturday evening, but this late in the year there would be few day-trippers, and the sea breeze would blow away some of the cobwebs that had enveloped him of late. He might even treat himself to fish and chips! In fact, come to think of it, he was famished! Dumping his suitcase in the hall, he checked his appearance in the mirror and made his way downstairs. What a funny old month it had been, he thought to himself as he walked towards the pier; the reassuring smell of vinegar and deep-fried batter hitting his nostrils as he turned onto Marine Drive. First, Gracie popping her clogs. Then that old letter turning up out of the blue. Shame there was no photograph inside. *What I'd give to see Jack's face again*. If only he could recall what he'd done with it.

Since being reunited with the letter, George had kept the envelope with him constantly. So, once through the entrance onto the pier, he headed to the nearest empty bench, retrieved it from the inside pocket of his overcoat and read the bit about the photo one more time. Try as he might to remember though, it still rang no bells. So, after a few minutes, he slid the letter back into his coat pocket – close to his heart once again.

Feeling a chill in the air, he breathed in deeply and was reminded of the reason for his stroll. Not for doughnuts or churros that was the prevailing scent of the pier these days, but a plate of good old-fashioned fish and chips. In late October it was far too cold to eat outside, so he pulled himself up from the bench and began to make his way to one of the restaurants further down the boardwalk. Of course, it wasn't just the cold that deterred him from eating *al fresco*. There were the seagulls to consider. Especially the one that seemed to have been eyeing him up ever since he'd walked through the entrance. Glancing over at the railings – on which the bird was sat – George became mesmerised by the panorama beyond. Beginning with the red doughnut ring of the i360 – effervescing in the night sky on the edge of Hove – he slowly took in the vista of brightly-lit hotels and bars that ran along the seafront up to Kemp Town.

More front than Brighton! he chuckled to himself, remembering what people used to say about Jack. And they were right. Always so confident and charming. Never seemed to care what anyone thought.

Looking over at the hotchpotch of buildings that made up the promenade, George tried to recall some of their favourite haunts.

Look, Jack. There's the road that goes up to what used to be Piggott's. Remember? Where we first met Paula? I can see her now. Pissed as a fart. Do give her my love next time you see her – the old lush! Turning his head to the left, George's gaze fell upon the Old Ship Inn, gateway to the Lanes, once home to a number of clandestine gay bars and cottages. *And over there was the Spotted Dog, where you used to try and kiss me when you thought no one was looking. Not that you would have cared if they had been!*

Being reminded of this tender moment, George felt a tickling sensation in his nostrils. Knowing what was coming, he reached for the handkerchief he always kept up his sleeve and blew his nose. But he wasn't quite ready yet to leave Jack wandering around on his own. He closed his eyes and continued his pub crawl down memory lane. *And that cocktail bar in Middle Street where they used to play show tunes all night. What was it called again?* George racked his brains, but nothing came to mind. *Bit on the posh side for us, wasn't it?* Unable to recall the name of the bar, George's thoughts drifted back to the present – and the rainbow-coloured pubs and clubs of Kemp Town, the city's new gay quarter, as it proudly and loudly called itself these days. Yes, even though the road had not always been a smooth one, George had to admit that they had come a long way since Jack's day. That being said, he couldn't help but feel a little

bit nostalgic for the past; when he was young, handsome –
and in love.

And then, all of a sudden, it came to him.

'The Argyle Hotel. That was it!' he shouted, out loud.

So loudly, in fact, that the seagull which had continued to
stare at him throughout, flapped its wings and flew off –
eventually landing on a life-size tableau of a bathing beauty
in the arms of weedy looking lifeguard. Of course, with no
tourists around to stick their heads through the holes above
the necks of the buxom bather and her rescuer, they both
remained spookily faceless. George smiled at the seaside
attraction before him. *At least some things haven't changed.*
And then, for the second time, in as many minutes, his grey
cells kicked into action once again. The photo in the letter.
'Hope you like the photo of us all on Paula's Birthday.'
It was Jack, Paula and Mancini sticking their heads through
one of those tableaux on the Palace Pier! He'd had a
modelling job in London that day and couldn't make it, so
they'd had it done specially for him. He also recalled why it
had got separated from the letter. He'd used it as a bookmark!
Jack's letter had arrived the morning of Churchill's funeral
at St. Paul's in London. Picking up the letter on his way to
the service at St. Mary's – arranged for Brightonians to pay
their respects to the great man – he'd had it with him in the
church. George's heart began to race. *Thank goodness no
one found it back then. It would have caused quite a scandal!*
Then he remembered what Ollie had said about the hymn
books. *'Not used since Churchill's funeral.'* Both the letter
and the photo had laid undisturbed for over 50 years. Until
Grace's memorial service. *Oh my goodness!* Suddenly a new
thought came to mind which made his heart beat even faster.
*What if the photograph of Jack was still there in the old
hymn book?* The prospect of seeing Jack's face again – the

face of his first love – made his stomach churn so much he completely lost his appetite for fish and chips; the only thing he hungered for now was finding that old photo. He knew it was the longest of longshots. It was over a week since the funeral. *Would those old hymn books still be out? Would the church even be open this late on Saturday?* He couldn't say. But what he did know was that he had to go there right away. Hurrying off the pier and past the old aquarium, he seemed to lose all sense of time and space; like an out-of-body experience, seeing himself from above. With this celestial image in his mind's eye, he prayed repeatedly that St. Mary's would still be open. *Thank God.* On reaching the AIDS memorial at the top of the New Steine – the church in sight – he saw that his prayers had been answered; the lights were on, someone was home.

Focusing on the kaleidoscopic colours of St. Mary's stained-glass windows against the pitch black of the huge building, George slowed his pace a little and by the time he reached the front door, he was calm enough to creep into the church unnoticed. Not least because the audience was engrossed in the string quartet that was playing in the chancel. Remembering where Ollie said he and his friends had been seated during Grace's service, George sneaked into the last pew and scanned its length for hymn books.

'Bugger!' he said, under his breath.

Littered only with prayer cushions and bibles, it was clear he was too late and not even St. Mary's beautiful windows could prevent the dark disappointment that gradually fell upon him. There was a momentary glimmer of light when he had the idea of asking Stephen Tindale, the verger. But then remembering that he was friends with Ollie, the flicker of hope was extinguished once more. The last thing he wanted was more questions about his past. No. He was going to have to accept defeat.

But just as he was about to give up the ghost, another one presented itself to him. Aware from the sound of clapping that the concert had reached its climax, George pulled himself up from the bench and was about to make his exit when he came face to face with someone else who would no doubt like to see Jack's face again.

Chapter Sixteen

Things that go bump
in the night

Saturday 26th October 2019 – 11pm –
St. Mary's, Kemp Town

After the warmth of the house, the October evening air greeted Ollie with a sobering slap across the face.

'Brrrrrrr! C'mon, Drew, cab's here,' he shouted to his boyfriend, who was still saying his goodbyes to the host and hostess.

'Stephen. Get a wiggle on,' he added in the direction of the Wicked Witch of the East. 'Or you'll be going home on your broom!'

The threat worked and minutes later all three of them, plus the hound, were making their way over the hill to Kemp Town and the promise of a nightcap at Stephen's flat on the back of St. Mary's.

'Are you sure, Stephen? Imagine what your parishioners will think if they see a werewolf being led into the vestry by a witch,' sniggered Ollie. But it was clear from Stephen's slurring that he was beyond caring.

'Just here is good, zank you,' he said to the driver as they reached the end of the alley that led to his rooms. And a few moments later, numbed by wine and several Hallowe'en-themed cocktails, the unlikely threesome and Mr Ben were making their way to Stephen's flat – until something stopped them in their tracks.

'I'm sure I turned the cellar lights off before I left,' said Stephen, more soberly.

'Ooooh, old-timers setting in already?' joked Ollie.

But before Stephen could reply, the light in the cellar was extinguished and the alleyway plunged into complete darkness.

'Shit! You were right. Looks like you've got visitors,' whispered Drew. 'C'mon, let's go back to the front and call the police.'

'Good plan,' agreed Stephen, turning back towards St. James's Street.

'At least you're not losing your marbles,' sniggered Ollie.

But it was too late. Suddenly the vestry door opened and flooded the alleyway with yellow light. Shocked by the unexpected turn of events, they all turned so quickly on their heels that they crashed into each other and ended up in a screaming mess on the floor. Narrowly avoiding being squashed beneath the mass of squirming bodies, Mr Ben broke free from Stephen's grip and in an attempt to protect them from the would-be attacker, began growling at the figure in the doorway. Though judging by the bloodcurdling cry coming from the silhouette, Ollie was certain that Stephen's late-night caller was more in fear of their own life to pose any real threat to him and his friends. In fact, there was so much howling and gnashing of teeth, it was difficult to know who realised first that none of them was actually in any danger at all.

'Miss Blythe!' cried Stephen, getting up from the floor and removing his pointy hat at the same time.

'Verger!' panted the figure in the doorway, gradually regaining her breath. 'You gave me such a fright.'

'Sorry, Miss Blythe. Hallowe'en party,' continued Stephen, giving his inebriated state away with a hiccup.

'Helloooo!' sang Ollie from the floor, suddenly aware that his joke in the cab about parishioners had come true. 'I'm Mr Hyde and this is Dr Jekyll.'

'Oh. Good evening Mr Hyde… Doctor.'

Oh God, she thinks he's an actual doctor, thought Ollie to himself.

'I'm so sorry, Stephen. I thought you were out. I did knock,' she said nervously, backing into the hallway to let them all inside. 'I was just looking for my glasses. I thought I might have left them in the cellar when I was doing the cleaning this morning.'

'Well, I see you found them,' said Ollie, removing his sideburns.

'Sorry?' replied the old lady, clearly a little confused by his comment.

'Your glasses,' he said, pointing to her eyes.

'Oh yes. My glasses. Silly me!' said Miss Blythe, glancing at her wristwatch. 'Gosh. Is that the time? I better be off. Nice to meet you, Mr Hyde. Dr Jekyll. Goodnight, Verger. Sleep tight. Mind the bugs don't…'

The final word was replaced with the slamming of the heavy wooden door, and the entrance hall was momentarily plunged into silence. Followed seconds later by howls of laughter from all three of them. Ollie was the first to regain his power of speech.

'My glasses… silly me… mind the bugs don't bite,' he mimicked, between more shrieks of laughter.

'She's absolutely priceless. Where did you get her from?' screamed Drew, who was next to find his voice.

'Came with. Part of the furniture,' replied Stephen, unable to form proper sentences, so breathless was he from laughing. 'Been a Friend of St. Mary's forever. Used to be a midwife at the Royal. Lives in sheltered housing next door. Got keys in case of emergencies. Good egg, really.'

After a final wave of giggles, the hilarity eventually subsided enough for Ollie to say what he was sure all of them were thinking. 'Lying, of course.'

'Too right. I wonder what she was really doing down there,' mused Stephen, walking towards the cellar door. 'C'mon. Let's have a look.'

Led by Mr Ben, one by one they climbed down the steep stone steps to the cellar. Cavernous but orderly, there was nothing about it that struck Ollie as particularly suspicious. Except, perhaps, an oddly familiar odour. The muskiness could have been the damp. The notes of sandalwood, some old lady perfume Miss Blythe was wearing. Then all of a sudden, it came to him. 'Bloody hell!' he exclaimed. 'That smell. It's aftershave. She's only had a bloke down here.'

'No wonder she made a sharp exit. The dirty old mare!' sniggered Drew, triggering even more laughter until the sound of Mr Ben wrestling with something at their feet caused them all to turn their attention to the floor.

'Oh, Benjino! What have you found now?' cooed Stephen, removing a pair of horn-rimmed reading glasses from his surrogate child's jaws. 'Any ideas?'

Chapter Seventeen

Desperate times, desperate measures

Monday 28th October 2019 – 11am – Think-U-Bator – Zarathustra Advertising, London

After being upstaged by Izzy on Saturday night, Cameron's week went from bad to worse. On opening the emails that had arrived over the weekend, it transpired that Bunny and her team were keen to 'bag the right celeb' for the gin campaign by the end of Thanksgiving. *Fuck!* thought Cameron, looking at the calendar on his laptop. *That gives us just over a month. Fuck! Fuck! Fuck!* With no new ideas on the table, there was only one thing for it. He would have to draw on the skills of the Director of Sexy Thinking, Damian King. The organiser of what other agencies called brainstorms, an agency as forward-thinking as Zarathustra didn't engage in anything quite so prosaic. No way! At Zarathustra, these sessions were known as Dream Catchers. There was even a special room at the agency called the Think-U-Bator, where two or three times a week, Damian King would gather together specialists from across the agency and perform the most brilliant exorcism of ideas using the standard tools of the trade; modelling clay, sticky notes and marker pens. Looked upon with mild amusement by most client service folk, these sessions were especially distrusted by agency Creatives, who on the whole seemed unconvinced by the idea that *ideas* could be had by anyone. *The very idea of it!* Surely ideas were magic. The children of genius minds. God-given to a select few. By which, of course, they meant themselves. Whatever was the genuine source of great ideas, on the challenge at hand, the river appeared to have run dry. So, a Dream Catcher session, it had to be – and Cameron to the Think-U-Bator, he had to go.

As the last one to enter the glass-walled room that was Damian King's dominion, Cameron made himself *un*comfortable in one of several brightly coloured beanbags skulking near the entrance to the room. *Jeez! Even the bean bags are trying to escape!* But it was too late to make a sharp exit. Counting everyone to be present and correct, Damian closed the door and readied himself to bring forth a veritable storm of ideas.

'Who will convince cool-hunting Soho-cialites to drink Rakewell's Gin?' asked the whiteboard at one end of the room. Beneath this was a refresher of the Think-U-Bator rules. The most laughable of which, Cameron decided, was that *there are no bad ideas, just ideas whose time had yet to come.* With everyone armed with this licence to say whatever popped into their heads for the next three hours, Damian kicked off the session by handing out a selection of coloured cards.

'What do you think of when you see the colour of the card you are holding? It could be an animal. An object. An event. Whatever it is, draw it on a sheet of paper. I'll give you two minutes,' said Damian, wiping the 'pool rules' off the whiteboard.

Being handed the colour purple, Cameron briefly flirted with the idea of drawing a scene from the film of the same name, before settling for an umbrella being showered with purple rain.

'Now turn to the person on your right and discuss how what you've drawn might solve the challenge,' announced Damian from the front.

Faced with the choice of either finding a few million to get Rihanna to front the brand or embarking on the equally expensive task of digitally resurrecting the Prince of Pop, Cameron struggled to see how his drawing was going to solve the challenge, which was still glaring down at him from the whiteboard behind Damian King.

Yet despite Cameron's reservations, the exercise turned out to be surprisingly fruitful. And what the suggestions scribbled on the small coloured squares stuck around the room lacked in quality, they certainly made up for in quantity. In fact, half a wall of sticky notes later, it seemed there was no shortage of ideas *whose time had come*. Next up was an exercise – or game as Damian preferred to call it – in which Cameron and his fellow prisoners had to wear spectacles representing a range of different people.

'I now want you to look at the challenge through the eyes of the person whose glasses you are wearing,' announced the Think-U-Bator's spiritual guru. Cameron paused a moment to take in the surreal image that presented itself before him. Wearing a pair of star-shaped spectacles was Katlyn, looking at the challenge through the eyes of *someone famous*. Thomas, in NHS-style specs, was summoning up the ghost of *someone who had died recently,* to help him crack the brief. And art director Rob, sporting a pair of 1950s shades, was looking at the problem through the lens of *someone you admire*. In the event, this turned out to be some sportsman Cameron had never heard of, not, as he had first assumed; Rob himself.

Cameron's pair, for the purpose of the 'game', belonged to *the last person he'd spoken to before entering the room*. Since the final thing he did before his incarceration was to talk to Mr Ben – who Alex had agreed to dog-sit for the day – for the second exercise, Cameron was now looking at the challenge through the eyes of a particularly feisty fox terrier. Once again, much to his – and he suspected everyone else's surprise – the 'game' proved rather productive and the company who came up with the idea of sticky yellow squares made another few quid.

'OK. For our last game I want you to feel for ideas,' said Damian, handing out different coloured pots of modelling clay. Reminded of Bunny and being involved in something faintly ridiculous, Cameron eased off the lid and breathed in the sweet and musty scent of nostalgia. *If my old man could see me now!*

'I know it sounds a bit daft...' said Damian, confirming what Cameron was already thinking, 'but this exercise will harness the power of one of the least used parts of our brains... the kinaesthetic lobe.'

Reassured by science, moments later eight fully-grown adults began kneading and pummelling their different coloured lumps of gunk into 3D representations of Soho. Cameron had to hand it to Damian; if he didn't believe this bullshit himself, he was a bloody good actor. What's more, even if the session hadn't caught any actual dreams, it had at least provided Cameron with enough 'seeds of ideas' to pad out a half-decent deck for the next meeting with Bunny and the CEO of Rakewell's Gin. Session over, Cameron gathered up the sticky notes that had received the most votes from the group and made his way over to King.

'Thanks, Damo. Great session,' he gushed.

'Thank you! For your energy and enthusiasm,' replied King. 'Some great ideas today, I think.'

'Aye,' replied Cameron backing out of the door. 'Let's just hope their time has come!'

Chapter Eighteen

One funny turn deserves another

After his few days away, George was looking forward to his Monday shopping ritual even more than usual. Not so much for the groceries he needed to buy. But for the gossip he hoped to pick up. After all, a whole week had passed since the funeral, so there ought to be plenty on offer. And from what he could see from his kitchen window, things had certainly moved on in his absence. Nice 'n' Naughty had removed the shrine to Grace from their window display. And Charles and Diana, no longer in mourning, had thrown themselves into Bonfire Night instead. He, naked, except for a jockstrap stuffed with bangers and rockets. She, in a red rubber firefighter costume, poised to hose him down. Yes, from where George was sitting, everything seemed to be back to normal.

So, where should he go first? Pharmacy perhaps? He needed to renew a prescription and it was always good for tittle-tattle of a medical nature. Or maybe the supermarket. Very little got past his friend on the fish counter, so there was sure to be something tasty to be had there too. He might even pick up some kippers for tea perhaps. Or maybe a nice piece of cod. Decision made, George was just about to make his exit when he heard his neighbour on the other side of the door.

'Hello. Anyone home?' said the muffled voice.

Halfway through pulling on his overcoat, he opened the door to find not one but two gentleman callers on his landing.

'Oh, hello boys,' he announced giddily, pleased to see that Ollie had his handsome new boyfriend in tow.

'What can I do you for today? More blasts from my shameful past? More bolts from the blue? More skeletons in my dusty old closet?'

Uttered so often over the years, these little phrases rolled as effortlessly off George's tongue as would lines in a well-rehearsed play.

'Actually, yes. Something like that,' said Ollie, awkwardly. 'But you're on your way out…'

'Gosh. Do I look that bad?' laughed George.

'No, I mean…'

'I know what you meant, dear. And yes, I was. But it's only the butchers, bakers and candlestick makers,' he said, backing into the flat and beckoning them to follow. 'Tea, coffee?'

'Tea, please,' replied both of them at the same time, following him into the kitchen.

'Please. Sit down,' said George, clicking on the kettle and gesturing towards the table in the bay window. 'So, what have you found *this* time?'

Drew took the magazines from his pocket and fanned them out on the table.

'These,' said Ollie.

Turning to see his younger self staring up at him from the cover of *CHAMPION*, George took a sharp intake of breath. Even without his spectacles, he recognised the yellow trunks and orange beach ball immediately; it was the photograph he'd had on his wall for years.

'It's you. Isn't it?' said Ollie, as the kettle boiled, temporarily enveloping George in a cloud of steam and buying him a few seconds to think about his reply. *It was him.* There was no point denying it. He'd put the cover in a frame in his hall, for heaven's sake. It was hardly top secret. In fact, thinking about it, he was quite flattered that they'd made the connection: that his wrinkled old self still bore some resemblance to the smooth-skinned younger version. Cloud dispersed, he emptied the water from the kettle into a teapot and joined them at the kitchen table.

'Where on earth …?' he began, gripped by a strange sense of déjà vu. 'Surely not an old hymn book!'

'Ha, no!' laughed Drew. 'An old desk this time. At Ditchling Rise Studios. What used to be Duke's Garage. Of course, it's changed quite a bit since Jack's day. Been converted into offices and workshops. I rent the space around the old mechanics' pit.'

'Goodness,' was all George was able to manage, still deciding how best to react. But as a seasoned performer, he was used to dealing with the unexpected and decided to respond as he would with any heckle: with humour.

'Oh, look at me. Couldn't throw a ball to save my life,' said George, now close enough to the magazine to see the front cover in more detail. 'And that grin. Cheeky little fucker! Still, I was quite a dish, wasn't I?' he said, cheerily stirring the tea leaves in the pot. *But why had they brought the other magazines*? He was pretty sure that issue of *CHAMPION* was the only one he'd ever appeared in. Then just as he was beginning to feel in control of the situation, the answer to his question hit him straight between the eyes. Staring up at him from the cover of *Adonis Body – Studies in the Male Physique,* there was Jack. Barely able to take it all in, George's mind went completely blank for a few seconds. And whether it was the abruptness with which he had stopped stirring the teapot, or the slight tremor in his hand as he reached across the table for the magazine, his reaction had not gone unnoticed.

'Oh my God! Is that Jack?' cried Ollie, pointing at the model who the magazine had chosen to call Brad. Still coming to terms with the unfolding drama, George wasn't sure how to answer. Of course, he knew he could have said that it wasn't Jack. *But why should he?* To lie would be to deny his existence. And he wouldn't do that. Not anymore. Not after everything that had happened in the last few days. So, gathering all the strength he could muster, he tore his gaze away from the handsome youth on the cover of the magazine and looked up at the handsome ones around his kitchen table. Ollie was the first one to speak.

'When we realised the boy on the front of *CHAMPION* was you, we thought maybe one of the other… er… lads… in the magazines might be Jack. And remembering what you'd said about the fire… and how you had no photos of him. Well, we just thought…'

George knew exactly what Ollie was trying to say. Quite sweet of them really. For a brief moment, he even flirted with the idea of telling the boys about the photo of Jack that he and Miss Blythe had recovered from the church on Saturday evening. But he quickly thought better of it. *Best to give them what they want and draw a veil over the whole affair.* Feeling more relaxed, a broad smile began to form across George's face.

'Brad my arse! Yes, that's Jack alright!' he said, finally.

'Jeez! Look at that bod. Fit as!' cooed Drew.

'Oh yes, the camera loved him alright. You can't quite see from that angle, but he had a right bona eek on him too!' laughed George, accidentally falling into Polari, the secret gay language that he and Jack used to talk.

'A real looker!' he translated, seeing the blank faces around the table.

'Ah, right,' said Ollie. Though George wasn't entirely convinced that either of them understood.

'All quite tame compared to what you can get away with these days. But we had to be careful back then. Being queer was against the law still, so this sort of stuff was the closest thing we had to gay magazines,' said George, slowly flicking through *Adonis Body* until he got to the centre spread.

'Ha!'

There was Jack again. Lying on his stomach with a closed copy of Blake's *Songs of Innocence and Experience* in his hands.'

'Now that's pushing poetic licence to a new level! Don't think I ever saw him read a book in his life!' Then feeling a little guilty for speaking ill of the dead, his tone became more defensive. 'He wasn't stupid mind. Street smart I think you'd say these days. It's one of the things I loved about him. And I did. Love him, I mean.' Seeing that it was the boys who were now stuck for words, George put the magazine to one side and poured them each a cup of tea. 'Well, well, well. What a funny few days it's been,' said George. 'First that old letter and now these. Thank goodness you asked me about Duke's.'

'I know. And how weird that Drew works there.'

'Oh no, dear. I don't believe in coincidences. These things happen for a reason,' replied George. 'Do you think I could perhaps…'

'Yes, of course. That's why we brought them round. In fact, something else has come to light that might interest you,' replied Ollie.

'Yes, dear?' asked George, happily reacquainting himself with the magazines.

'Something to do with your friend Paula.'

George looked up from the magazine.

'*Paula?*'

'Her attic to be precise,' added Drew. 'A trunk of old costumes. And a reel of film.'

'Yes, something about Yanks,' continued Ollie, picking up the thread.

'Yanks?' repeated George.

'Yes, apparently that's what's scratched on the side of the tin,' continued Drew.

All of a sudden, the horror of what they were saying finally hit home. Gasping for air, George stood up, looked at them both, then feeling faint, fell back down again. Temporarily plunged into darkness by the clouds of memories closing in on him, after a few seconds he became aware of something flapping in front of his face. Not the wing of a large bird, as he had originally thought, but Ollie, wafting the wooden tray on which he had just carried over the tea things. *Oh God. What had the boys said? A reel of film? In Paula's attic? Oh God. Oh God. Think, Georgie, think.* As his breathing gradually steadied, question after question swirled around inside his head. *What could possibly be on there? Wasn't everything destroyed in the fire? What was he going to do?* One thing was certain, he needed some time alone to gather his thoughts. Breathing almost back to normal, he sighed deeply until he was able to speak.

'Sorry, my dears. All these blasts from the past have quite done me in. I think I need to lie down,' he said weakly, as Ollie put the tray back on the table. Thankfully, the boys seemed just as keen to make their exit. So, with no further questions, they said they hoped he would feel better soon and said their goodbyes.

Hearing the door close behind them, George picked up *Adonis Body*, walked the few steps into the lounge, and sank into the nearest armchair. His mind still whirring, he vaguely remembered Paula saying she'd worked at some film studios after leaving Brighton. It's probably not anything to do with him and Jack. But that title. That certainly rang a bell. Something about Yanks, didn't Ollie say? *Yanks... Yanks are.... Yanks are coming...* Exhausted by the morning's revelations, George closed his eyes and fell soundly asleep.

Chapter Nineteen

Camera. Lights. Achtung!

Saturday 6th February 1965 – 8.30 am – Coleshill Abbey, Rottingdean

George couldn't quite remember how he'd ended up asleep in Jack's lap. But judging by the pounding behind his eyes, there was no mystery as to *why* he was there. Lifting his head up from the warm nook provided by his boyfriend, he gradually became aware that he was not the only one awake. How else could the aroma of fried bacon be drifting up the stone staircase? Careful not to wake Sleeping Beauty, he gently removed Jack's hand from his shoulder and placed it where his head had just been. Jack coughed, but otherwise he remained in the Land of Nod. Eyes slowly adjusting to the semi-darkness, George re-familiarised himself with the room. In front of him there was the tea-chest with now empty wine bottles placed on top. In the far corner were a few bags of clothes they'd brought from the car. And next to them was some of the kit they'd be using later. Conspicuous by her absence was Paula. Just then he heard a car door slam from somewhere in the near distance. Remembering the moonlit snog that he and Jack had stolen at the top of the tower a few hours earlier, he decided to return to the floor above to see what the commotion was outside. With a banging hangover, the climb up to the turret took longer than it had done the night before when he and Jack seemed to have flown up in a matter of seconds. Likewise, the view that greeted him when he opened the door was different from the one he remembered. Disorientated as much by the shrieks of the seagull he'd disturbed by his sudden arrival at the top of the tower, as he was by the bright light of day, it was hard to believe it was the very spot where, only a few hours before, Jack had drunkenly thrust his tongue into his mouth and sucked the red wine from his lips. Horny as hell, the sex had been hurried and hot; Jack's taut, muscular body bucking uncontrollably as he shot his load. There had been a few more kisses – more affectionate than before – and then they were dressed and back inside. The memory of it fired up George's heart rate and made his head hurt again. It also made him smile. And it was only Saturday morning. He still had two whole days with Jack to look forward to. Breathing in the cold air, he ran his fingers through his thick blond mop and walked over to the gap in the turret wall where the seagull had been resting.

As he suspected, the noise he'd heard earlier was Paula leaving the car in which she had slept. What surprised him though was in which car she seemed to have spent the night. Not the Morris, as he had assumed. But the Daimler. How odd. *I wonder how she wormed her way in there.* Though they'd all had quite a skinful. Reminded once again of the pounding in his head, George headed back towards the bacon smell where he thought he might also get his hands on some headache tablets.

'Ah, buongiorno, ragazzo,' beamed Mancini, seemingly unaffected by the previous night's drinking. Or maybe he'd necked a few pills already.

'Er, morning,' replied George, climbing gingerly down the last couple of stone steps into the ground floor where Jack's boss was frying bacon and eggs over a camping stove.

'Pass me my jacket, will you?' he said, pointing to the back of one of the chairs arranged around a large kitchen table in the middle of the room.

'Fa un freddo cane!'

'Sorry?' enquired George.

'It's dog cold!' Mancini translated. 'Freezing!'

'Aye, you're not wrong there,' agreed George, penny finally dropping. 'Cold as a witch's titty me gran used to say.'

Just as George was in the middle of recounting his gran's old saying, Paula pushed open the heavy wooden door to the ground-floor room – narrowly avoiding tripping up on the car blanket in which she was wrapped.

'Did someone mention titty?' she cried, stumbling into the table.

'Yes. I said it's as cold as a witch's…' replied George.

'Fackin' right. And I should know, I've met a few in my time!' she said, howling at her own joke just as Jack appeared at the bottom of the stairs.

'What's all this talk about titties?' asked Jack, clutching his head. 'Please. Please. Titties ye not!' This impersonation of a comedian from the telly caused them all to fall about laughing. 'At least until the banging in me head's gone away!'

'This will sort you out, sunshine,' said Mancini, handing Jack a plate of bacon and eggs. Better than any headache tablets, the fry-up worked wonders on all of their hangovers and minutes later they were ready to get on with the filming.

'OK. Let's get the outside shots done for *Yanks* while it's still light. For this one, the client wants Jack to be our GI Joe and Georgie our German POW. He's got a thing for blond boys and bondage. Apparently, you as that cowboy tied to the totem pole went down a storm with his friends,' said Mancini, coiling some rope around his wrist.

'Whip crack away, whip crack away!' cackled Paula.

'Alright, Calamity Jane, let's save the wisecracks for after the filming, shall we?' chastised Mancini. 'OK. Ragazzi. Go get your uniforms on, and me and Paula will meet you at the bottom of the field in 10. First scene is GI Joe tying the Kraut's wrists together behind his back.'

'Great! More fucking rope burns!' was all George could muster, rolling his eyes to the ceiling.

'Don't worry, Georgie boy,' said Paula, holding what counted as a storyboard. 'You can get your own back in the next one. *Whore and Peace* it's called. You get to play Napoleon. Nice cossie too!'

'A real *bona* part!' laughed Jack, dropping into Polari to annoy Paula, who'd never managed to get the hang of it. But she was already busy setting up.

'What's the first one called again?'

'The Yanks are Coming!' shouted Mancini, over his shoulder.

'Ha. You'll just have to lie back and think of Deutschland, Georgie boy!' snorted Paula, as she scratched the title on the side of a circular blue tin.

'I'll lie back and think about that flat we want to get on St. James's Street,' he said to Jack, as he followed him upstairs to get ready for their first scene.

Chapter Twenty

The gunpowder plot thickens

With Drew snoozing quietly next to him, Ollie took the opportunity to catch up on his socials, which in the last week had, by and large, been about the upcoming Bonfire Bonanza. In fact, in the last 24 hours alone, Cameron had kept his Facebook page for the event burning with all manner of Bonfire Night themed posts. Photos of baked potatoes and honey-drizzled sausages. A recipe for a ginger cake – called parkin – handed down to Alex from his Aunt Vera. It sounded a bit sickly, but Ollie had 'liked' it anyway. There had been videos of spectacular firework displays. And several of the *You've Been Framed* variety showing displays that had gone *spectacularly* wrong. And most intriguing of all, a selection of public information films from the 1970s explaining how to deal with a range of dilemmas such as 'why you should never return to a lit firework' and 'what to do with pets during the festivities'. *Just how stupid were people in the 70s?* thought Ollie, after watching one such film. Being one of the first to tick 'going', Ollie had not only seen all of Cameron's posts but the tirade of messages from fellow guests, too.

'So excited!' ran one from Stephen, who, as the owner of a particularly feisty mutt, Ollie suspected was secretly praying for rain and a quiet night in by the fire. Though thanks to the public information film, he would at least know how to protect Mr Ben's ears from the upcoming aerial bombardment.

'Sure it'll go off with a bang!' Izzy had written. *Yeah right. Hoping for a whimper more like.* Though having had time since her Hallowe'en party to look at that old reel of film, the 'bang' to which she was referring could perhaps be whatever she'd discovered.

But no matter what might have been the true meaning behind his friends' messages, Ollie for one was looking forward to the party. Not least because he had chosen the occasion to reveal the true identity of 'Brad'. And best of all, as far as Ollie was concerned, was that so soon after Izzy's fancy-dress party, Cameron had decided against costumes and requested his guests wear nothing fancier than a hat and scarf. In fact, with so little preparation required for the evening's event, Ollie and Drew had spent the afternoon in bed enjoying a firework display of their own. And by the time St. Mary's could be heard chiming seven o'clock, not even the lure of honey-drizzled sausages and Aunt Vera's parkin had proved tempting enough to prise them out of bed.

'Fuck. We'll be late for the party,' said Ollie.

'Slow down, boyo. The party starts when we get there!' replied Drew, yawning.

'If you say so, *boyo!* But I'm not so sure the sausages will hang about. C'mon, we better get a move on or the only food left will be salad.'

'Jeez. You certainly know how to put the fear of God into a Welshman, dun you?' joked Drew. But the threat had worked, and minutes later they were strolling up St. James's Street discussing the next big event on the social calendar. Les Tableaux Vivants.

'So, Oscar or Bosie?' asked Ollie.

'Oh God, yes. That tableaux thingy.'

'Vivaaaants,' said Ollie, exaggerating the word in his Black Country drawl.

'Well, you've totally nailed Oscar's posh accent,' offered Drew, to get the ball rolling.

'Ha. Very funny. But seriously…'

'Yes. I think it's important to be *earnest*,' replied Drew, this time raising a smile from his boyfriend. The fact was that with their shaven heads, neither of them bore much of a resemblance to either Bosie or Wilde. *And wigs were definitely out of the question.* 'I seem to remember Bosie wearing a lot of cream in the film,' said Drew, thoughtfully. 'How about I wear my old cricket whites?'

'Cricket whites! Really! You played cricket?'

'Yeah, back in Cardiff. Hit quite a few sixes in my day. You not a fan?'

'Hell no! Gymnastics was the only thing I was any good at.'

'Aye, you're not wrong there.'

'Thanks. Not too bad yourself,' replied Ollie, before returning to the earlier theme. 'I had a massive crush on the captain of the school team, though. What I'd have done with him behind the cricket pavilion!'

'Well, maybe I can dig out my whites the next time you come around.'

'Mmmmm, yes please,' said Ollie, beginning to wish he'd stayed in bed a bit longer. But seeing the explosion of colour in the sky overhead and hearing the familiar 'crackle-bang-ooooh-aaaah' immediately after, he was reminded of how much he loved Bonfire Night. And this year there was the update about the magazines and the reel of film to look forward to as well. *Who knows what 'crackle-bang-ooooh-aaaahs' they might cause!*

'Ollie! Drew! You're here at last. I thought you'd had a better offer,' said Cameron at the door, before leading them to the patio at the rear of the house.

'You've missed most of the fireworks, but I think there might be some food left,' he shouted above the piercing scream of a Catherine wheel somewhere behind him. 'There's definitely some of Alex's parkin!'

'God help us!' whispered Drew under his breath. Though on reaching the kitchen it appeared that God had indeed helped them, and they happily gorged themselves on honey-drizzled bangers, baked potatoes, mushy peas – and even a slice of Aunt Vera's famous ginger cake. Stomachs lined, fireworks fired, and glasses charged, the conversation finally turned to the Mystery of Coleshill Abbey. And in particular, the much-awaited update about the reel of film. Not least, Ollie suspected, by Izzy herself.

'Well…' she began, once the core group were in earshot. 'It's early days still. And we need to check their authenticity. But what I *can* tell you is that, like those magazines Ollie and Drew found, the films *are* early examples of gay pornography.'

Pleased to have been name-checked, Ollie joined the rest of his friends, with the notable exception of Cameron, in congratulating Izzy for her discovery. Yet it was clear from the frenzy that followed that what she had unearthed had created more questions than answers.

How many films were there? What were they of? And most importantly of all, were George and Jack in them? One by one, Izzy tried to fill in the blanks. There were eight films in all. Much like the magazines, they were the usual mix of homoerotic fantasy. Soldiers and sailors. Masters and servants. And sporting types like the boxer and his coach in the humorously titled, *Boxing Clever*. What was more, based on the cover of *CHAMPION*, Izzy was fairly certain that one of the 'actors' was George. But since she had no idea what Jack looked like, she couldn't say for sure if he was the other boy in the films. Though as it turned out, being familiar with his likeness might not necessarily have been much help anyway since the cameraman, or woman, as was more likely the case, had been careful to maintain the actors' anonymity throughout. Yes, there were plenty of close-up shots of body parts, but clever camera angles and lighting meant that faces were more difficult to make out.

'Of course, at this stage, we can't be certain. But I really think the collection is very significant,' she enthused to her audience.

Given George's reaction to hearing about the discovery of the reel, this update from Izzy, while tantalising, was no great surprise to Ollie. What was unexpected though was the historical importance she attached to them. And he was not alone.

'Really? Why do you say that, Isobel?' enquired Cameron, stifling a yawn. Obviously still furious about Izzy's discovery, thought Ollie, recognising his friend's trademark response to being upstaged.

'Ooh. Lots of reasons, darling,' fizzed Izzy, excitedly.

'Oh, Isobel. How you spoil us! Just one will do,' Cameron shot back. 'We're not all as clever as you, darling!'

Although used to their sparring, the backdrop of whistles and bangs from other bonfire parties in the neighbourhood added an extra dimension and Ollie happily lit the blue touch paper and stood back.

'Go on, Izzy, don't keep us in suspenders!' he gushed.

'Well…' she continued. 'For one thing, films like these are extremely rare. I've discovered from my research that they were usually produced for private individuals, and so those that do exist most likely remain in private collections.'

'Sounds like you've really struck gold, darling!' added Cameron, congratulating his nemesis on her discovery.

A second 'darling'. Surely, she must know that Cameron is mocking her.

'Historically speaking, yes... I think they're very important,' continued Izzy, pointedly in Cameron's direction.

'Especially for Brighton.'

Crikey! She's played her ace! The Brighton Card! The widely accepted view amongst Brightonians that as long as a thing benefits their beloved city, then it is, without question, a good thing. Accordingly, as expected, all nodded in unison.

'Some of the first films ever produced were made here, so it's a fantastic addition to Brighton's cinematic heritage. And queer history too. Especially as our city has one of the largest LGBTIQ+ communities in Europe,' she beamed proudly. Not even Cameron could argue with that!

'In fact, the museum thinks there's a book in it. A documentary even,' added Ken.

'Well, maybe,' said Izzy.

'Oh, is there a problem?' enquired Cameron. Ollie couldn't help feeling his tone was less than sympathetic.

'Mmmmm... well... as part of Paula's estate... technically speaking... we... Ken and I... own the rights to the films,' Izzy explained, in some obvious discomfort.

'But the museum feels we should get George's blessing too,' added Ken.

'In a nutshell, yes...' said Izzy, turning to Ollie before continuing. 'So, I was wondering if...'

'Ah...' interrupted Ollie, guessing where Izzy's request was heading.

Being reminded once again of the fainting fit that was triggered by the mention of the old reel, Ollie didn't think there was much chance of Izzy being blessed by George anytime soon. So, with that in mind, he decided it was time to bring everyone up to speed with his own detective work.

Yes, he could confirm that the boy on the cover of *CHAMPION* was definitely George. No, he didn't seem at all shaken or surprised. In fact, after the initial shock, he'd actually been quite upbeat about it. Flattered even.

'And the most exciting thing of all,' said Ollie, saving the best till last. 'It turns out that poetry-reading Brad – on the cover of *Adonis Body* – is, in fact… Jack!'

'Fantastico! That's brilliant,' gushed Izzy, excitedly. 'We'll now be able to say whether he is the other boy in the film too!'

'Ah… mmmmm… however…' continued Ollie, preparing the way for the news that Izzy would find less *fantastico*.

He was right. After a brief summary of George's reaction to the discovery of the film and how Ollie thought it unlikely that the old man would give his permission to use it, a noticeably crestfallen Izzy simply said, 'Oh!' and left the huddle. Looking around at the circle of disappointed faces, Ollie could see that it was a feeling shared by them all; with the exception perhaps of Cameron, whom he thought seemed a little buoyed up by his update.

'Such a shame,' said Ken. 'She'd really set her heart on that documentary.'

'I was so looking forward to seeing Brad get his kit off too,' added Adam, rather predictably.

Fearing the fate that often befalls the bringer of bad news, Ollie racked his brains for some distraction.

'At least we have Maria's and Meena's housewarming to look forward to next month,' he said, finally.

'Oh yes, how's it all going, ladies?' cooed Cameron, happily picking up the theme. *Too happily, in fact,* thought Ollie. But with the spotlight off the messenger, and the chances of him getting shot being markedly reduced, he welcomed Cameron's enthusiasm to pick up the baton. *But where had Izzy gone?* Ollie stepped back from the group a little. Oh, there she was, scribbling something down at the dining-room table. Intrigued, but also satisfied she was OK, he tuned back into the update on the upcoming Winter Tableaux Vivants.

'A dead baby!' were the chilling words he heard from Meena, on his return.

'Oh God, darlings. It was like a horror film!' recalled Maria dramatically. 'I've never seen Meena run so fast!'

'She's right. I screamed the place down,' said Meena, confirming her wife's account of the discovery, which thankfully turned out to be a case of mistaken identity. What Meena had feared was entombed in a blanket at the back of their log-shed, was, in fact, hundreds of empty jars of baby food. Of course, this had been no random discovery. Ollie knew from the most recent 'renovation bulletin' that following the discovery of the love letter, and its mention of their new home, the girls had been on the hunt for clues dating back to the abbey's infamous recent past. And while looking up chimney breasts and under loose floorboards had drawn a blank, it appeared that since the last *snooze*-letter, there had been a find; the old log-shed, in which they plan to stage their Tableaux Vivants, had rewarded them with a stash of old jars, a baby cot and a pile of rotting papers dating back to the mid-1960s.

Ollie was about to ask about the newspapers when he noticed Izzy at his side, beckoning him to join him in the dining-room.

'Sorry to drag you away, darling,' she said to him once they were out of earshot. 'I just wondered if you'd give this note to your neighbour. I know what you said. But I just thought if he knew just how important the films are, he might reconsider. Especially as him and Jack are barely recognisable in them.'

'Worth a go, I suppose,' replied Ollie, beginning to feel guilty for bursting her bubble.

'I've mentioned the museum too... might sway him.'

'Yes, good idea. I'll pop it under his door when I get in,' replied Ollie, relieved that for once he wouldn't be required to rake over George's past in person; a little note of his own would suffice. He did feel he owed her this at least. Mostly he enjoyed the rivalry between her and Cameron, but it was unkind of his friend to be so obviously pleased about George's reaction to the films. It wasn't good for Cameron to have it his way *all* the time. If George could be persuaded to go public with the films, it was good for queer history. And as Izzy had said, good for Brighton too. *And what Brightonian could argue with that!*

Chapter Twenty-One

On the same (Bettie) Page

Tuesday 5th November 2019 – 11am – Brighton Museum

If Izzy was going to remember Bonfire Night 2019 for anything, it would not be for the burning of a chap called Guy Fawkes. No. This year the event would be associated instead with the incineration of her latest academic ambitions. She knew that without George's permission to go public with the films, the story of Brighton's clandestine gay porn industry would be pretty lacklustre. *What a waste.* If only George had gone the same way as Grace, she thought to herself guiltily. *No. Stop it, Izzy.* But why, oh why, did her dreams have to go up in smoke in front of Cameron-fucking-MacIntyre? With that bitter taste in her mouth, she dragged the digitised films from her desktop onto a USB stick and placed it into the circular tin which had contained the original film. No sooner had she pressed down the lid than she got a call from reception.

'Oh, hello, Izzy. I have a visitor for you. A Mr Gibbons.'

She couldn't believe her ears at first. But against all the odds, a few minutes after putting down her phone, George Gibbons was sat in front of her. At least she assumed it was he. Truth to be told she barely recognised him from the grainy films. For one thing, the George in front of her had significantly more wrinkles. For another, he was wearing quite a few more clothes. Adopting her most professional manner, Izzy resisted the temptation to make the obvious comment and smiled at him sweetly across the desk.

'So, Mr Gibbons. How can I help?'

'Oh please. Call me George, dear,' he said, retrieving a folded sheet of paper from the inside pocket of his jacket. 'It's about those films you wrote to me about in your letter.'

'Yes, of course. What would you like to know?' said Izzy, heart in her mouth. He seemed friendly enough. But remembering what Ollie had said about how George had reacted to the discovery of the films, she had to consider the possibility that he was there to demand them back!

'Well, I think my reaction when I heard about them might have given the wrong impression. To Ollie, I mean,' he continued.

'Oh!' said Izzy, breathing out a sigh of relief.

'If what you said in your letter is true. Just some silly old films I made a lifetime ago. What harm could it do to let more people see them? Quite tame, in fact, from what I can remember. Hardly the sort of thing that would scare the horses. Not these days anyway!'

'No, not at all,' said Izzy, beginning to feel a little giddy.

'And to be honest. I'd quite like to see my old self again. And Jack, of course. The other chap in the films.'

So, it was Jack. Fantastico! Izzy tried to remember what she'd hurriedly written in her note. What was it that had softened George's resolve? Made him eager even. Was Jack the reason? It's possible. But had she even mentioned Jack? It had all happened so quickly; she couldn't say for sure. In any case, whatever George *thought* was on the films counted for nothing. If he was going to give his permission, there was only one thing for it. She decided to strike while the iron was hot.

'Would you like to see them now?' she said, retrieving the USB stick from the tin in her in-tray.

'But I thought…' George began to say.

'Oh, we've had them digitised,' interrupted Izzy, suddenly animated by the turn of events. 'The reel of film has been sent to the museum's conservators. The quality has deteriorated quite a bit over the last 50 years, I'm afraid. Especially your faces. Though Paula was pretty good at obscuring your identity with clever camera angles anyway. I guess you had to be careful back in those days.'

'Yes…' said George, bashfully.

'But don't worry…' she continued, sensing his disappointment. 'I'm confident we can return them to their original glory. With a little TLC.'

'How clever. And yes, I'd love to see them again,' said George.

After deftly inserting the USB into her laptop and pressing play, Izzy turned the screen around to face George – and crossed her fingers.

To her great relief, she saw no dread in his face. Far from it. As the films rolled, he smiled and giggled. In places, he even laughed out loud. It was obvious that George was enjoying seeing his old self – and Jack – again. Could she hope that his change of mood might come with a change of heart? She said a little prayer. Not least because, only moments before, she'd wished the old man dead!

'Oh my. We were quite a couple of lookers, weren't we?' he said, turning the screen back to Izzy. 'But why would the museum be interested in a few old…?'

Knowing this was her chance to get her dreams back on track, it was a challenge to which she rose with aplomb.

'Well, George. The thing is… historically speaking, these films are *very* significant… particularly in terms of queer history.'

George stared at her in silence.

Realising this line of argument wasn't exactly rocking George's boat, she dropped the academic approach and tried a different tack.

'The fact is. The museum wants to make a film about you!'

'A film?' spluttered George, in stunned surprise.'

'Well… a documentary really. But who knows after that?'

'No!' said George incredulously. 'But who in their right minds would want to see a load of dodgy old porn films?'

'Oh gosh! Lots of people. You'd be surprised. Since finding that old love letter of yours, it's all my friends have been talking about for weeks. And the people at Hove Museum are really excited too. In fact, they think you could be the British Tom of Finland! The Brighton Bettie Page!'

'No!' exclaimed George, touching the cravat tied around his neck as if it were a string of pearls. Of course, thought Izzy, why hadn't it occurred to her before? What could be more persuasive to a performer than the chance of a moment in the spotlight? The involuntary clutching of his non-existent necklace certainly seemed to suggest that her visitor was moved by the prospect of fame. But still he paused. Saying nothing, he undid his cravat and folded it neatly on his lap. Finally, after a good half a minute, he looked her squarely in the eye and said, 'And these are the *only* films you found?'

'Yes, that's right. There were a load of old costumes and theatrical props. But this was the only reel of film. We've had a proper clear out since we found this.' She was so close. She couldn't risk losing him now. 'But there's more than enough to make a documentary. And once more people get to see them, I'm sure you will have quite a fanbase! I mean, the camera obviously loved you…'

It was time to play her winning card.

'…and Jack,' she said finally, reaching across the table for George's hand. 'Wouldn't that be a fantastic way to celebrate his memory? To celebrate your relationship. Your love!'

Locking her brown Spanish eyes on his pair of Brighton blues, Izzy held her breath.

'Oh, well then,' said George, grabbing Izzy's hand to complete the healing circle across the table. 'What the heck.'

'You mean you'll do it?' squealed Izzy, dropping the professional act for a second. 'You'll let us go public?'

Finally, after what seemed like a lifetime, the answer she'd been waiting for – if not the actual words – left George's lips.

'You bet your sweet ass, I will!'

Chapter Twenty-Two

Pure Gin-ius

Wednesday 6th November 2019 – 4pm – Zarathustra Advertising, London

'The gin that made the 60s swing!' announced Cameron, reading the first slide of the presentation being streamed into the wood-panelled room where he'd delivered the Rakewell's Gin pitch two weeks before.

Since hearing they'd won the business, the agency had been busy adding flesh to the bones of the campaign and today was Cameron's first chance to show Donald Hunter, the brand's CEO, how things had progressed. First up was the new colour palette. Gone were the teal, olive and mint greens of yesteryear. Rakewell's new wardrobe would be orange, purple and gold.

'If Rakewell's was going to rise like a phoenix, it was going to have to dress like one!' said Cameron, clicking onto the slide showing the proposed packaging. From the smiles he saw at the other end of the video screen, he was pleased to see that Donald and his team were lapping it up.

So far, so good.

Next there was the new typeface. A curvy font inspired by posters for the sort of films that seemed to capture the optimism of the decade in which the brand had first appeared. Movies that usually featured stick-thin girls in mini-skirts, skipping around London to a jaunty 60s pop beat – and plots that were often thinner than the girls themselves.

A cursory glance at the grins on the faces of his audience reassured Cameron that once again they liked what they saw – and he rattled through the remaining slides about the 'look and feel' with the breezy confidence of one of the aforementioned films.

But there was still the thorny of issue of who should front the relaunch. About this, he was less certain. Though thanks to the recent Dream Catcher session, he did at least have some ideas to present. So, after running Rakewell's CEO through the design recommendations, Cameron moved onto the question of possible brand ambassadors.

'OK. Let's move onto the biggie. *How can we make the swinging 60s relevant to today's gender-fluid Soho-cialites?*' asked Cameron, reading the headline from the intro slide to the next part of his presentation. He noticed Hunter whispering something to Bunny, but decided it was nothing important and continued with the section about who they thought could front the relaunch.

The first potential brand ambassador was an actor who had recently played a double-agent in a spy drama set in 1960s Russia. A James Bond type. Just as handsome and fit, but being on TV, he would probably be about half the cost. The idea had arisen from the exercise in the Think-U-Bator around colour in which a red card had led the group to come up with a bunch of people associated with communism, the Cold War and infamous traitor Anthony Blunt. In the storyboard, the actor receives a secret delivery of Rakewell's Gin which he promptly decants into empty bottles of Russian vodka: the gin, his only connection to the decadent world beyond the Iron Curtain.

Cameron did his best to sell the concept, but he could tell from Hunter's face that he wasn't buying it.

'But what's the big idea, Cam?'

'The *big* idea?' Cameron repeated, not sure which made him cringe more. The casual – and uninvited – shortening of his name, or the inclusion of the industry's favourite prefix.

'The *big* idea?' Cameron repeated, followed by a *big* intake of breath.

For a split-second, the *big* idea in Cameron's head was shortening Hunter's name to Don and frisbeeing the of storyboard in the direction of the CEO's *big* fat stupid head on the 42-inch plasma screen. But remembering that the Rakewell's Gin relaunch was a *big* opportunity to pull in some *big* bucks, he decided to be the *bigger* man and play nice instead.

'The *big* idea, Donald? In a word, the big idea is... nostalgia,' said Cameron, confidently.

'Oh, I see,' began Hunter. 'But aren't the Russians a bit anti-gay these days? I'm not sure that'll go down well with our *gender-fluid Soho-cialites!*' he said, smirking.

Was he mocking Cameron's description of the target audience? It sounded like it. *So that's what they'd been whispering about.* He did have a point though. The Russians weren't exactly flavour of the month with the gays. Thank goodness he had a couple more ideas to present.

Next up was a lesbian comedienne from Ireland, who had first shot to fame in the 90s with an innuendo-charged game show, before going on to become one of TV's most sought-after hosts. The suggestion of this celebrity had been arrived at by looking at the 'challenge' through the eyes of Stephen's cantankerous old fox terrier. Exactly how this Think-

U-Bator exercise had led them to the middle-aged Irish comedienne, Cameron couldn't remember. Perhaps he had regaled his team with the anecdote about Mr Ben trying to grab Adam's rubber devil horns at the recent Hallowe'en party? Horny Irishman-funny story. Whatever was the source of the idea, the Director of Sexy Thinking, Damian King, was convinced it was an idea *whose time had come,* so it seemed churlish not to unleash it on the world. Especially as the comedienne in question had been born in the 60s and was, Cameron reassured his audience, hugely popular with the LGBTIQ+ community to whom the gin would primarily be marketed.

'Get the gays, and the kids will follow!' was Hunter's rather predictable response.

'Exactly, Donald! Exactly,' agreed Cameron, clicking on a montage of the comedienne's best bits that he had inserted into the presentation.

'Yeah, she's pretty funny,' acknowledged Hunter after watching the video. But Cameron sensed there was a but coming.

'But...' added Hunter, on cue. 'Isn't Irish a bit too... whisky?'

'Or Guinness,' chipped in one of his sidekicks.

'Got any gay English comedians born in the 60s?' suggested Bunny.

Sadly, he didn't. And with only one more potential brand ambassador to present – a wee laddie who recreated scenes of urban life in and around Soho in textiles – Cameron was beginning to feel a little despondent. Quite appropriate since the idea of using the artist had come about during the exercise in which Damian had handed out pots of modelling clay and asked everyone to 'feel' for ideas.

'The big idea here is about weaving the brand into the fabric of Soho,' said Cameron, heading off the expected question at the pass, while he flicked through a few slides of the artist's work.

'We thought we could commission him to do a series of pictures inspired by London in the 60s. In purple and orange fabric.'

'Mmmm. I kind of like it…' began Hunter. *Fuck. At last, we're getting somewhere.* But what Cameron thought was light at the end of the tunnel, soon turned out to be a train coming the other way.

'…but isn't it a little bit too arty for us, Cammy?'

OK. Enough was enough. Hunter may well be the *big* cheese. But Cammy! Really! That's it. No more Mr Nice Gay. Cameron finally snapped.

'Well, at least we know what you dinnae want – *Donny!*' Cameron shot back at the old goat. 'Nae commies. Nae Irish. And certainly, nae arty types!'

Despite being reminded of a sign in the window of a 1960s guesthouse, Cameron managed to stave off a smile long enough for Bunny to correctly deduce that they had reached an impasse.

'OK. Well, how about we focus on what we do want? I'm sure you guys will crack it soon. You always do in the end!' she trilled, in that reassuring way that clients seem to swallow. Thankfully, her *gin*-tervention did the trick and Cameron and his team were bought some more time. But with no more ideas – *big* or otherwise – up his sleeve for now, the meeting was drawn to a close, and the plasma screen turned to black.

'Well, that went well,' said Katlyn.

'More like a car crash than a meeting,' huffed Thomas.

'Fucking Yanks,' added Rob, happy to leave the witty repartee to his writer.

But as usual, it was Cameron who found the right words for the occasion.

'Glemonade, anyone?'

Chapter Twenty-Three

They saw, they came

Thursday 14th November 2019 – 7.30pm – Hove Museum, Hove

'Bloody hell, is it mid-November already!' said Ollie, as the bus went under the illuminated SPARKLE… FAIRY… TWINKLE signs strung across North Street.

'I know!' agreed Drew. 'It'll hardly be worth taking the tree down if it gets any earlier!' He wasn't wrong. In keeping with a fairly recent tradition, once the unsold fireworks had been removed from supermarket shelves, it was now the custom to begin decking the malls with boughs of holly. Or fake snow and tinsel as was more often the case these days.

Of course, the fairy lights weren't the only sign that the season to be jolly was upon them. *Or proof, should any more be needed, that there was nothing quite as camp as Christmas.* Ollie had already visited Ye Olde German Christmas Fayre in Jubilee Square that week. And as he noticed from the adverts on the side of every bus that they passed from North Street up to Hove Museum, Brighton was about to be hit by an avalanche of snow-filled movies. The highlight of which for Ollie was always the Christmas screening of *It's a Wonderful Life*. Another time-honoured tradition that, fingers crossed, he would be sharing this year with Drew. Yet it was not James Stewart that had enticed Ollie out on a chilly November evening. The reason was instead, a special screening of a new acquisition by Hove Museum that was deemed historically significant to both Brighton and cinematography itself. In short, tonight was the premiere of the films that Izzy had found in her attic. Ollie could barely contain his excitement. And it was clear from the small crowd that had already gathered outside Hove Museum that he wasn't alone.

Getting out of a cab just as their bus pulled in were Adam and Alex. And Ollie was certain that the campervan he'd seen from the bus earlier on, belonged to Meena and Maria. As for Cameron, he was already inside, chatting to Izzy's son, Josh, and the Korean boy from the Rainbow Hub who'd been handing out flyers for Grace Davidson's candlelit vigil.

'Look!' said Ollie, pointing the trio out to Drew. 'Perhaps he's Josh's boyfriend.'

'Make a cute couple if he is,' replied Drew.

It was true, thought Ollie, focusing on Josh. The spotty teenager that Izzy had introduced him to a few months before had blossomed into quite an attractive young man. There was definitely more of Ken than Izzy in his face, but in the brightness of the entrance hall, Ollie could see that Josh's once greasy skin had a definite Mediterranean glow about it. In fact, seeing him afresh, Ollie thought he reminded him of someone famous. Justin Bieber was it? Or perhaps one of the 1D boys. He was about to ask Drew when Adam came bounding up beside him with a more familiar enquiry.

'Who's the hottie with Cameron and the cute Korean fella from the Rainbow Hub?'

'Don't! That's Izzy and Ken's lad.'

'Noooo. He's gorgeous!'

'Adam! He's 17! Stop it!'

'Don't tell me! Tell Mr Flirty Knickers over there,' quipped Adam, just as Cameron erupted into a fit of giggles in response to something Josh had said to him. But despite Adam's comment, Ollie couldn't help but wonder, from his beaming smile and the way he kept shoving his floppy fringe over his right ear, that any flirting going on was coming from Josh – not Cameron.

Whatever the direction of the attraction, the sudden appearance of Izzy put paid to their chat and minutes later everyone had been ushered into a large room on the ground floor that had been turned into a makeshift cinema for the evening. Ordinarily used as the café, tables had been pushed to one side and chairs laid out in rows. At the far end of the room was a projector screen and a lectern. Placed in the middle of these, on a small platform, were two chairs and a table. Taking his seat in the front row – reserved for Izzy's closest friends – Ollie placed his hat and scarf under the chair and readied himself for the main event. He didn't have long to wait. No sooner had he put his phone on silent than the lights were dimmed, and the title of the evening's event appeared on the screen. *BOYS ON FILM: Brighton's pioneering role in queer cinema.* It certainly sounded intriguing. But once the coloured circles flickering across the screen were replaced by the image of a boy in a hooded dressing gown and matching red boxing-gloves, Ollie was under no illusion why he had trudged across town that evening. *Boxing Clever* had begun.

He watched in awe as the lad beat the living daylights out of a punch-bag suspended from the ceiling. Left. Right. Jab. Right. Left. Left. Jab. Of course, by now he knew the boy's identity. Not Brad, but George's dearly departed lover, Jack. What he hadn't expected though were the noises that accompanied the scene. Assuming the films would be silent, he was pleasantly surprised to hear the sound of fists on leather and the occasional grunt as Jack danced around the bag. Even though they were mostly out of sync!

'Wouldn't want to get on the wrong side of that one, would you?' he heard Alex whisper to Cameron, as the camera panned around to reveal more of the boxer's muscly legs and calves.

'Oh, I dinnae know about that!' replied Cameron, under his breath.

He's right, Ollie thought to himself. Even though the film was pretty grainy, and you couldn't make out Jack's face at all, he remembered the boy's profile from the cover and centre spread of *Adonis Body* and was immediately turned on. Shifting in his seat to accommodate the tightening in his underwear, he returned his gaze to the screen just as Jack pushed back the hood of his gown. Ollie fidgeted a little bit more. *Oh shit, this is getting embarrassing.* Though the awakening in his crotch caused by the opening scene was nothing compared to what happened when Jack sat down on a bench and let his gown fall open, revealing a glistening six-pack. Ollie could barely contain his excitement. And judging by the sound of other audience members re-arranging themselves in their seats, it was obvious he was not alone. *But where was George?* Noticing Jack nodding to someone off-camera, Ollie didn't have to wait too long for his answer. Too blurred at first to make out, the back and shoulders of a blond-haired youth carrying a bucket and towel, slowly came into focus. Once in shot, there were audible mutterings of acknowledgement in the audience as a very young George Gibbons began drying Jack's hair with the towel. As he did this, the camera swung around behind

Jack before cutting to a close-up of George's hands removing Jack's gum-shield. Punching over, the sound effects gave way to a classic porn soundtrack of elevator-muzak mixed with the occasional groan. On the screen, George began removing Jack's gloves. Careful not to reveal their faces, the camera slowly panned around for another close-up shot of George's hands untying the laces. Gloves placed to one side, Jack slipped his arms out of the robe and let it fall to the floor. There was a cut-away close-up of George's hand reaching into the bucket for a yellow sponge. Small droplets of water fell on Jack's legs and shorts as George slowly dragged the water-drenched foam over his lover's stomach, pecs and shoulders.

'Here we go,' whispered Drew, squeezing the fleshy part of Ollie's leg above his right knee. Already rock-hard, Ollie managed to discreetly place his hands in his lap just as George began a trail of kisses from Jack's shoulder down to his six-pack. Caught up in the moment, the sponge dropped to the floor. There was a close-up of George's hands pulling down Jack's shorts and another of the bulging jockstrap beneath. Accompanied by a Mexican wave of seat gymnastics to Ollie's left and right, it was obvious that the passing of time had done little to diminish the erotic charge of this burlesque floor show. And there was more to come! Jockstrap down by Jack's ankles, George got to work. At least that is what Ollie imagined was going on, for the next scene was a close-up of Jack's hands gripping the edge of the bench. Followed moments later by the familiar multi-coloured circles, Ollie was suddenly aware that it wasn't only the film that had reached its climax. As the full enormity of his little mishap began to sink in, the rest of the room greeted the end of *Boxing Clever* with a more dignified appreciation of the film and Izzy made her way to the stage.

Absent from the enthusiastic clappers, of course, was Ollie himself, whose hands at this precise moment were needed elsewhere; scrabbling under his chair for something to cover the wet patch he knew had appeared on his crotch. Hat and scarf safely placed on his lap, he took a deep breath and hoped to God it would dry before they left the auditorium.

'Thank you. Thank you. Gosh. I wasn't expecting that,' said Izzy.

Neither was I, thought Ollie. *Orgasming over my septuagenarian neighbour. In public, for Christ's sake.*

'Thank you so much for coming,' continued Izzy.

If Ollie had managed to side-step her first comment, the second was more difficult to ignore, and he couldn't help but let out an involuntary squeal. Thankfully, just as he thought he was going to be caught in the beam of one of Izzy's frightening glares, a new distraction grabbed her attention. Suddenly, out of nowhere, a large seagull landed with a thud on the sill of a window to his left, the blind of which had not been entirely pulled down. Momentarily thrown by the uninvited guest, after a second or two, a visibly shaken Izzy took a deep breath and continued.

Phew! Saved by the gull!

Chapter Twenty-Four

Pun-ography

Reminding her of Ken's comment about waking Paula's dead spirit, the appearance of a seagull staring at her from a side window caused Izzy to freeze for a moment. But noting that the applause had died down to an expectant silence, she dismissed the silly thought and began her presentation.

'*Boxing Clever* is just one of several movies recently acquired by Hove Museum that I will be sharing with you tonight. Shot on cine film, time has taken its toll on the quality of the originals and these are currently with our conservators, being restored to their original glory. The digitised copies I will be showing tonight, however, do have the advantage of not requiring a noisy mechanical projector, which some of you may remember was always a part of the viewing experience.' Judging from the chuckles that Izzy heard around her, she assumed that there were a few in the audience who did. 'But don't worry, ladies and gentlemen, we don't expect you to watch in silence. Thanks to our technical department, just like *Boxing Clever*, all the films I will be showing you tonight will be accompanied by appropriate sound effects and music. I do hope you enjoy the results. But first, a little bit of historical background.'

Relieved to have made it to her presentation, Izzy pressed her thumb against the clicker and moved onto her first slide.

'The Hollywood of England,' she announced grandly, clicking onto a sepia photograph of an old film-set. 'Not as far-fetched as you might think. In fact, in the 1890s, over a hundred films were shot using locations in Brighton and Hove. Films such as *Scene on Brighton Beach* by R.W. Paul and the evocatively titled *Boys Scrambling for Pennies Under the West Pier* by Esmé Collings.'

Click. The sepia image was replaced by a screenshot from the aforementioned film, featuring a group of urchins – presumably scrambling for pennies. Greeted with a chorus of 'oohs' and 'aaahs', the appreciative response gave Izzy a much-needed boost and she started to gain momentum.

'Notable amongst the early film-makers associated with the city is George Albert Smith. *A Visit to the Seaside* made by the Natural Color Kinematograph Company in 1908 is thought to be the first film made in colour using Smith's Kinemacolor technique.'

Click. Unable to find an image from this film, Izzy instead treated the audience to a photo of the great man himself. Sitting behind a bureau surrounded by various tools of his trade, the rather handsome Mr G.A. Smith looked every inch the genius he probably was. That being the case, she did think the 'phwooar' she heard from the front row was a tad disrespectful. Recognising the Irish accent, her gut feel was to cast a withering look in Adam's direction. But fearing it would encourage him even more and also because she wasn't entirely sure where he was sitting, she ploughed on instead.

'One clear sign of the importance of the film industry to the city was the establishment of the Brighton and County

Film Company in 1911 – with the financial backing of the racing driver, S.F. Edge. Changing its name shortly afterwards to BRIGHTONIA, amongst its productions made in Brighton were *The Motor Bandits* in 1912, and *East Lynne* and *The Grip of Iron* in 1913.'

To maintain the audience's interest throughout her synopsis of the rise and fall of Brighton's movie industry, Izzy peppered her presentation with screenshots from the various films that she mentioned along the way. *Had their interest been maintained?* Owing to the glare of the spotlight, she couldn't say for sure. But the stifled yawn that she heard from the front row certainly cast some doubt on the hope that it had. Rattled a little by this, she made a daring detour from her well-rehearsed script.

'Not long 'til the next film!' she cooed into the bright light, causing a ripple of polite laughter from the crowd. Relieved, she moved onto the section about the rebirth of the British film industry.

'As a result of strict censorship in the United States, by the end of the 1950s, Britain once again became the place where writers and directors could push boundaries. Especially in the genre of sex.'

At the mention of sex, the auditorium was suddenly alive with the sound of creaking chairs and shifting bodies. Her audience was literally sitting up and listening. Reassured by this, Izzy motored on with renewed enthusiasm. And even though the next few slides featured nothing remotely pornographic, she knew that the room would not be disappointed since most did feature shots of Brighton from a series of movies filmed in their beloved city. There was the Pavilion, North Street, Brighton Station. Even Edward Street.

'…before the Nazis and our town planning department razed it to the ground,' joked Izzy, prior to moving on to talk about one film of particular note called *Genevieve* – starring Kay Kendall and Kenneth More. Less obscure than some of the other titles she had mentioned earlier, Izzy was keen to focus on the film since not only did it feature several crowd-pleasing shots of Madeira Drive, the Old Steine and Brunswick Square, it also gave her the chance to underline her previous point about strict censorship in the American film industry.

'Apparently, the film ran into problems because of a scene in which an actress asks if she can "spend a penny",' said Izzy, explaining that references to toilets were especially taboo in the US at that time. A point that caused the expected sniggers that Izzy knew all Brits were hard-wired to emit on the mention of anything lavatory related.

'By the 1960s, horror movies from the Hammer stable and comedies like those produced under the *Carry On* franchise – together with the gritty realism of 'kitchen sink' dramas like *A Taste of Honey* and *Look Back in Anger* – put Britain back in the spotlight.'

Looking up at the screen, Izzy gave herself a mental pat on the back for being able to accompany this last nugget of wisdom with a shot of Dora Bryan and Rita Tushingham from the film *A Taste of Honey*; arguing a few feet away from an *actual* kitchen sink. Although Izzy knew this film had no genuine connection to Brighton, she was thrilled to add that Bryan had once owned Clarges Hotel on Marine Parade, which was used as an exterior location in *Carry On At Your Convenience* – triggering a further tinkle of amusement.

'By the swinging sixties, increasingly relaxed censorship laws for film and theatre in the UK provided the impetus for even more experimental movements on the fringes of film. And it is to these I now wish to turn.'

Whether she heard someone in the audience say, 'Thank feck!' she couldn't be certain. But in keeping with the aforementioned comedy classics, she decided to *Carry On Regardless*.

'The recent discovery of a collection of early gay films, shot and edited in and around Brighton, is, I believe, one of the most important examples of the genre to come to light in recent times. Produced in secret, usually at the request of wealthy clients in the United States, films of this nature that were not destroyed by the censors most probably remain in private collections. Why *this* collection ended up in a house in Brighton, we'll never know. But thankfully, about the people behind these extraordinary films, we do know a little more.'

Click. Suddenly the room was flooded with light as a colour photograph of a ruddy-faced woman with short peroxide blonde hair appeared on the screen.

'Belonging to a woman called Paula Buckthorn, a relative of my husband, in fact, the films were discovered only very recently. As I said, how Ms Buckthorn ended up with them is unclear. But what we do know is that she was behind the camera on all the films that I will be showing you tonight.'

Izzy paused for a moment to take a sip of water.

'And that's not all we have discovered. Thanks to the detective work of some local history buffs, we also know the identities of the actors. And that their affections for each other continued off-screen, too.'

Another sip of water.

'But more of that later.'

She paused and clicked onto the next slide.

If the mention of 'sex' had awakened her audience's interest, the image of George and Jack in white sailor uniforms had them transfixed. Though their profiles were obscured by a thick veil of smoke, the contours of the tight-fitting trousers were not. In fact, such was the hubbub caused by the sight of their youthful buttocks, Izzy even had to raise her voice a little to make herself heard.

'After whetting your appetite with *Boxing Clever,* I would now like to introduce you to *Sailor Blue*... an homage to Jean Genet's 1947 homoerotic novel *Querelle de Brest*...' Replaced with a shot of George tied to a totem pole and Jack dressed as a whip-wielding Native American, Izzy continued to pick her way through the script against the barely hushed whisperings of the crowd. Especially in the front row.

'... followed by *Wild, Wild West*... where our blue-eyed cowboy is about to be the subject of some Wild West S&M!'

This image was swapped seconds later by one in which a Roman soldier was wrestling with a man dressed in white robes. Face obscured by his helmet, the soldier's taut body gave his identity away as Jack, while the laurel-crowned blond boy was obviously George.

'And *The Rides of March*.' Buoyed up by the excitement caused by the series of saucy images, Izzy decided to go off-piste. 'In which Caesar falls victim to Brutus's weapon.'

Waiting for the laughter to subside, Izzy took the opportunity to take another sip of water before bringing the section to a close.

'Lying hidden for many years, it is likely that, aside from me and my colleagues, you are the first to set eyes on these films for over half a century. So, without further ado, let us dim the lights once more and roll the film.'

Stage lights off, the glow from *Sailor Blue* illuminated the boys in the front row. Or more specifically, their constant crossing and uncrossing of legs. *My goodness! What slaves those boys are to their desires,* thought Izzy, smiling to herself in the darkness. And spotting Cameron's strategically placed coat, it took all of her strength not to laugh out loud. *That'll teach him to wear such tight-fitting suits!* What had Josh called him last week? Oh yes, Mr Skinny Pants.

Reminded of her son, she took advantage of the light to see where he was sat. Partly to make sure he wasn't too close to Cameron – she hadn't failed to notice them laughing together earlier – and his comment about him thinking Cameron was 'pretty hot for an old fella' was still quite fresh in her memory. The other reason she was keen to locate Josh was that he had agreed to present her 'surprise guest' with a thank you gift at the end of the interview.

Distracted by the undulations of the front row and trying to locate Josh, before she knew it, the films had ended, and her assistant had returned the room to its previous chiaroscuro; the audience in darkness, and she, once again, in the light.

'Thank you, ladies and *gentlemen*. I am so pleased that you are enjoying these films as much I have been doing,' she said, pointedly, in the direction of the boys in the front row. 'Especially as we are now at the point in the evening when I would like to introduce a very special guest.'

Blindsided by this unexpected turn of events, the audience became noticeably agitated, some twisting their heads in the hope of seeing the surprise guest at the back of the room.

'Earlier tonight I said that we knew the identities of our two film stars,' began Izzy, momentarily pausing for effect.

'Well, we can do better than that.'

What before had been hushed speculation, now erupted into excited chatter.

'Yes, that's right. Please join me in welcoming on stage one of the stars of *Boxing Clever* and the other films you have just seen. A lifelong resident of Brighton and the man that some of you may know as local celebrity, Bette Y'Sweet Ass. Please put your hands together for the one and only – Mr George Gibbons.'

Chapter Twenty-Five

Guest of dis-honour

Thursday 14th November 2019 – 8.30 pm – Hove Museum, Hove

Still to replace his lost spectacles, the walk from the back of the room took longer than George would have liked. *And what if, horror of horrors, the applause dried up before he got to the stage!* He needn't have worried. Clapping wildly in a way that reminded him of a demented seal, Izzy managed to rekindle the dwindling flames of appreciation for his final few steps. Yet despite the second wind of applause, he still felt uncharacteristically nervous. It was more than his spectacles he was missing; without the usual armour of panstick, wig and padded bra, he felt less confident all round. Thankfully, once in the spotlight, he regained a little of the regal presence he enjoyed as Bette and gestured to the audience to calm down. *I'm only an old porn star turned drag queen. Nothing to see here!* At least that was what he was thinking as Izzy's assistant fitted a microphone to his lapel. This done, he put on a pair of pink-hued sunglasses and smiled appreciatively in the general direction of the audience. Not, in fact, chosen to protect his eyes from the unkind glare of the spotlight, but rather the shades were the only prescription glasses he had until his new ones were ready for collection. Though in one sense, they did seem to him as rather appropriate. After all, weren't the memories about to be disturbed going to be better appreciated through tinted lenses?

'So, George,' began Izzy. 'First of all, let me say thank you for agreeing to be here tonight.'

'Oh gosh. Don't thank me, dear. Thank my doctor – and the pills he gives me. I'm surprised I'm here myself!' replied George. 'I'm just sorry Bette couldn't join me tonight. I'm afraid she's not feeling herself.' Testament to the claim that while you can take a queen out of drag, it's more difficult to take drag out of a queen, George paused and looked towards the audience to deliver the punchline. 'For a change!'

While there was no cymbal to accompany his quip, it was clear to everyone that Bette *was* in the room after all. Izzy waited for the laughter to subside and navigated the interview back to safer waters.

'So, what's it like to see your old self again after all these years?'

'Oh! It's dreadful, dear. I've never felt more ancient!' shrieked George. Then seeing an opportunity to steer the interview off-course again, he turned back to the audience and – in a voice and manner that was all Bette – saucily purred, 'Wasn't I a dish?'

Floundering for a moment, Izzy smiled, looked down at her list of prepared questions – and continued.

'As Bette Y'Sweet Ass, you are Brighton royalty. But we know very little about George Gibbons. Could you tell us a little about him please?'

'Of course, dear. I thought you'd never ask.'

True, George's interrogator was no Parkinson, but this was the closest he was going to get, so he was going to milk it for all it was worth. Move over Davis, Midler and Lynch, there was a new Bette in town. And she was loving every second of it.

'Well, my dears. If you're all sitting comfortably, I will begin,' said George. 'Me and Jack…' But no sooner had he started, than he stopped mid-sentence, placed his right palm to the side of his mouth and turned to the audience. 'He's the ugly one!' he whispered loudly into the darkness, triggering another ripple of laughter. George waited a few moments and then picked up where he'd left off.

'Me and Jack met in '64. I remember because I'd just celebrated my 18th birthday the week before. It was at a beach party in Hove. Jack was wearing a pair of skimpy black trunks. Very racy back then, you know! But that was Jack all over. He just didn't care. And I loved him for that.'

'So, would you say you were lovers?' asked Izzy.

'Lovers! I should cocoa, dear!' guffawed George. 'You don't get all that—' he waved behind him at the screen '—from method acting.'

'No. I suppose not. So, what happened? To Jack, I mean?'

'I'm afraid he died, dear. Not long after these films were made. A car accident, somewhere between here and Rottingdean,' said George, rather matter-of-factly. He and Izzy had rehearsed the bare bones of the interview beforehand, so talking about Jack's death did not throw him as much as it might have done otherwise.

'So tragic,' said Izzy. 'I mean, finding someone special is hard enough. But being gay in the sixties – when it was still illegal – it must have been almost impossible. And then to have him snatched away from you like that… It's absolutely heartbreaking.'

Despite the rehearsal, this stroll down memory lane suddenly made George feel vulnerable again, and he paused a moment to collect his thoughts.

'Yes, dear. It was. Utterly so. He was my first ever boyfriend. Head over heels I was,' replied George, before taking a sip of water. 'But it was years ago... and besides, these days I choose heels over heads every time!'

Punctuating his bon mot with as high a high kick as he could manage from his seated position, the audience responded accordingly, and the interview was pulled back from the emotional cliff edge.

'So, could you tell us a little more about how you came to be making these films in the first place. I mean, did you have to audition?' continued Izzy, as the laughter subsided.

'Well, it wasn't advertised in *The Stage*!'

'No, I don't suppose...'

'We were approached. Jack and me. In a pub that was popular with our sort. It's still there today. Not queer anymore, I don't think. *The Spotted Dog* it was called back then.'

George heard a few mumbles of recognition from the audience.

'It's one big room now. But back then it had a front and back bar which you got into from a side corridor. Jack and I preferred the front. It was where the day-trippers would wander in, and we'd always place bets on how long it'd take 'em to realise they were the only straights in there. Of course, it wasn't obvious like it is today. There were no rainbow flags or half-naked barmen.' Seeing an opportunity for a joke, George reached for his glass and turned to the audience.

'More's the pity!' he said, raising an eyebrow and taking a big gulp of water.

'Sounds charming. So, tell us about the night you were approached by a stranger in the Spotted Dog.'

'Oh no, dear. Not a stranger. Far from it. Very much known to us both, in fact.'

Consummate professional, George knew this was a cliff-hanger moment and paused to take another sip of water.

'It was Jack's boss! The owner of the garage where Jack worked as a mechanic.'

'Oh, I see. Please tell us more.'

George removed his shades and scrunched up his face as if to say to his audience, *hold the line caller – I'm just putting you through to the distant past.*

'It was summer. I know that because we had our costumes and towels with us. We must have been swimming and stopped off for a quick one…'

Hearing a snigger from someone in the front row, George stopped mid-sentence.

'A drink, you cheeky sod,' he said towards the audience. 'Dirty lot you've got in tonight, dear. I thought Hove was supposed to be the posh end of town!'

Even Izzy got this joke and gave a little peal of schoolgirl giggles before George picked up where he'd left off.

'Really! Now, where was I? Oh yes. A little *drink* before heading home to change. We usually went a bit more upmarket on Saturday evening, so the Dog would have been early.'

'And was Jack surprised to see his boss in a… I know you wouldn't call them gay bars back then, but you know…' queried Izzy.

'Heck no. We saw him in the Dog all the time. It was how Jack came to be working for him at the garage in the first place. The Dog had a… how can I put it? A reputation for attracting the town's more colourful characters.'

'Colourful?'

'Yes. Jack's boss was Italian. His family had moved to England after the war. His dad was in construction,

I think. But that wasn't for Mancini – that was his name – Michael Mancini. Motors were his thing. Fast ones especially. In fact, he was quite well known in racing circles before he took over Duke's; the garage that's now called something else.'

'Ditchling Rise Studios,' interjected Izzy.

'Yes. That.'

'So, tell us more about Jack's boss – Michael Mancini.'

'Well, it was obvious to us that he batted for our team. But he was very discreet. Three-piece suits and trilby hat. I don't think anyone outside of the scene suspected. And besides, not *everyone* at the Dog was queer. It attracted people who wanted to appear edgy. If you catch my drift.'

'You mean he was a bit of a gangster?'

'Ha!' laughed George. 'He was hardly Brighton Rock! But he did seem to know a lot of shady people, yes.'

'How fascinating. Please, go on…'

'In fact, on the evening in question, he was carrying a load of magazines for one of these contacts. What they used to call 'physique' magazines.'

To emphasise the inverted commas, George made little bunny ears with two fingers on each hand. From the laughter that followed, George assumed the audience knew what he meant. But just in case…

'Bodybuilding and that sort of thing.'

And then just to make absolutely certain.

'Porn. Basically.'

'Oh yes, I came across some of those in my research,' added Izzy, excitedly.

'Mmmmmm…'

Assuming from the giggling in the front row that the audience needed no help with that one, George decided to let Izzy's accidental double-entendre pass without comment.

'Yes. In fact, he was quite open about it. They weren't illegal or anything like that. Just a little bit, you know, under the counter.'

'But he had a successful business. Why take the risk?' asked Izzy.

'Well, the money for one thing. It was a nice little earner. In fact, I think it was quite a *big* little earner. But it was more than that. It brought him into contact with lots of influential people. And you always got the idea it was a means to an end with him. Always had his eye on a bigger prize.'

'You mean the movies?'

'Yes, dear. That's right. He was keen to branch out into something a little more adventurous than bodybuilding magazines. The next big thing in porn was going to be film. And he knew lots of people who would pay top dollar for it too. All he needed were a couple of willing models.'

'And…' began Izzy.

'Yes, dear. Audition over. Signed, sealed, delivered. We'd got the job.'

'And the films we are showing are the result. Which brings me nicely to part two of tonight's show,' said Izzy, gesturing to someone in the distance who George assumed was the colleague who had fitted his microphone. Moments later the room was plunged into darkness once again, and the titles to *Master & Servant* rolled across the screen. Well, this is fun, thought George, as he watched his younger self help a very aristocratic-looking Jack out of his eveningwear. He had to take his hat off to Paula and Mancini. How they had managed to recreate a gentleman's boudoir with just a potted plant, a full-length mirror and a changing screen, was ingenious. *I bet none of those dirty old sods we did this for would have guessed in a million years that it was all done in that draughty old storeroom at Duke's!*

Just then – about the same time that his younger self began undoing Jack's dress-shirt – George became aware of a light in the audience. My word! Someone's bloody filming it on their phone. Cheeky buggers! One for the wank-bank, no doubt. Perhaps Izzy was right about me being the British Tom of Finland. Well, George of England! If only Jack could have been here to see this, he thought to himself, as the titles for the final film of the evening began to roll; another Roman-themed affair called *Slaves of Rome* in which Jack was getting all steamy with his bath-time slave boy. Filmed once again in the glamorous location of Duke's Garage, George smiled to himself as he recalled how pleased Paula had been to get her hands on the discarded backdrop from a production of *Antony and Cleopatra*. With that hung up over the garage's stained-glass windows, who couldn't fail to be transported back to Ancient Rome! There was no faking the steam though. But with the original films being silent, the sound of the boiling kettle remained in George's memory only. Not that it would have mattered anyway since Izzy's people had added the sound of a snake-charmer to the film in an attempt to recreate the ambience of a Roman bathhouse. George wasn't entirely sure whether it had worked, but before he could make up his mind, the film reached its predictable climax, and the haunting pipe tune was replaced by the noise of a hundred hands clapping their appreciation.

'Ooh, I could get used to this,' said George, rising from his chair and giving a bow.

'You deserve it. It's been a long time coming,' replied Izzy.

Seizing the opportunity, George quickly turned to the adoring crowd and cried out, 'Speak for yourself, dear!'

Too focused on her next question, Izzy continued with her script.

'So, in my talk earlier, I mentioned a woman called Paula Buckthorn. My husband's aunt and the person whom we have to thank for the survival of this incredible collection. Could you perhaps…'

'Of course, dear. She was another regular at the Dog. Another misfit. Right gob on her too, from what I remember. Ooh, sorry, dear,' said George, interrupting himself.

'Oh, don't worry. She was still pretty outspoken when I met her,' said Izzy, reassuringly.

'Well. Jack and her got on like a house on fire. She adored him. Just like the rest of us. I mean,' he said, gesturing to the screen, 'what's not to love!'

'Yes, quite,' giggled Izzy, politely.

'In fact, we were all very close once upon a time. Until Jack's accident. We sort of lost touch after that. I still saw her occasionally around Brighton, but we moved in different circles. And to think, all that time, she had those films in her attic. Not really her sort of thing, if you know what I mean,' said George, winking at the audience.

'Yes. But thank goodness she did. And thank *you* for letting us share them with everyone tonight.'

'The pleasure was all mine,' replied George graciously.

'And thank you to everyone for making it out tonight on this chilly November evening,' said Izzy to the audience.

'But before you head home, George, we have a little surprise for you. My son Josh – Paula's grandnephew, I think he'd be called – would like to present you with a gift as a memento of those heady days.

'Josh!' cried Izzy, beckoning someone to join them on stage.

'Oh, how kind,' said George appreciatively, expecting a bouquet of flowers or something similar. *What a nice way to end the evening*, he thought to himself. And he was at least half right. For while the appearance of a young man rising from the darkness into the bright spotlight did indeed make for a memorable finale, by no stretch of the imagination could what happened next have been described as *nice*.

'No. It can't be!' cried George, removing his pink shades to get a closer look at the olive-skinned freckly-faced youth coming towards him.

'Jack? Is that you?'

But before the boy had got close enough to hand over the gift. George gasped. Fell back into his chair. And passed out.

Chapter Twenty-Six

Cry baby

Sunday 7th February 1965 – 10am – Coleshill Abbey, Rottingdean

While Jack remained dead to the world, for the second time in as many days, George woke up with a banging hangover. The wrap party – as Mancini called it – had been quite a drunken affair and he couldn't actually remember how, or when, he'd made it upstairs. At least this time he'd had the foresight to grab several items from the costume trunk to create a makeshift bed – before he was too sozzled to care where he fell. Paula, on the other hand, had been less prepared. Though having fallen asleep in the trunk itself, she also had the wardrobe department to thank for her bed. In the half-light of the room, George could just about make out her blonde hair against the green canvas used for the tent scene in *Whore and Peace*. And from the sound of her snoring, the bearskin busby he'd worn in *Rear Sentry* – had made a comfortable pillow. Until…

'Fackinell!'

She was awake. And she was not happy.

From what George could decipher from the words in between the torrent of buggers, shits and *fackinells*, was that she thought she'd spent the night with a dead cat. A mistake that George assumed had been rectified when moments later she began laughing hysterically.

'Shhhh. Keep yer hair on, y'dozy dyke, my head's proper bangin',' whispered George, in an effort not to wake Jack. 'What time is it anyway?'

'How the fack do I know? Who d'you think I am? The fackin' talking clock? I'll tell you what time it is, Georgie boy. It's time you got a fackin' watch,' she barked at him from the trunk.

But before he could ask her to lower her voice again, Paula's tone suddenly changed.

'Oh, hang on a minute. That's weird.'

'What is?'

'Mancini's Rolex. I'm wearing it.'

'What, his watch?'

'Yes.'

'His Rolex!'

'Yes! His fackin' Rolex!' she said, raising her voice again, causing Jack to stir beneath the trench coat. 'Are you deaf as well as fackin' stupid?'

'Yeah right, pull the other one. It's got bells on,' replied George, just as Jack's head appeared above his makeshift cover. Yawning and stretching at the same time, he sniffed the air and picked up the theme.

'Well, it's time Mancini got breakfast on, that's all I can say. I could murder a bacon buttie. Can't smell anything, can you?'

Assuming Paula was pulling their legs about the watch, the subject was dropped, and they all sniffed the air in the hope of picking up a faint whiff of bacon.

'Nope, naffink,' said Paula in answer to the previous question. 'Maybe, he's not up yet. I'll go and see what's what.'

With that, she pulled herself out of the trunk and felt her way to the door. Satisfied that breakfast was still some way off, Jack returned to the warmth of the trench coat he'd slept under, mumbling something about needing a piss.

'Rolex my arse. She's off her bloody rocker that one,' George said to Jack's back as he too slid under the makeshift bedding and slipped his arm around his boyfriend's waist. Though it was clear to the few who knew about them that Jack was the butch one, under the sheets, he was far more vulnerable and loved being cradled. As such, George was none too pleased when Paula came crashing back into the room.

'He's gone!' she cried, breathless from running up the stairs.

'Gone to get some fuckin' bacon I hope,' came the muffled reply from Jack.

'No! For good!'

'For good?' asked George, confused.

'Yes. He's left a letter. Look!' she said, throwing it at George and running out of the room in floods of tears.

'Fuckin' hell. I think we better get up and see what she's on about. C'mon, Jack. Wakey, wakey.'

'For fuck's sake. I really do need a piss now.'

Moved, George suspected, more by his bladder than Paula's waterworks, Jack pulled on the cloak he'd been sleeping under and wearing just that, his drawers and his unlaced boots, followed his distressed friend down the stairs. George, meanwhile, was left clutching the piece of paper that Paula had thrust at him moments earlier. Despite the shafts of light seeping in through the holes in the rug they had put up at the window, the room was still too dark to read the letter. But noticing the glint of the metal buttons on the guardsman jacket that went with Paula's makeshift pillow, he tiptoed his way over to the source of the twinkle. Discovering that the trousers were close by, he took the split decision to don the entire ensemble – including the busby – and joined his friends, downstairs.

After dealing with his own waterworks, it appeared that Jack had moved his attention to Paula's, rubbing her shoulders in silence as she sobbed inconsolably with her head on the table. Glancing over at George without the slightest acknowledgement of his get-up, Jack gestured towards the letter.

'So? What's he say?'

Expecting the letter to be read out, Paula stopped sobbing, lifted her head from the table for a moment – and then collapsed into a flood of tears once again. Perhaps it was the sight of him wearing what she'd earlier mistaken for a dead cat that had set her off? George couldn't be certain, but just in case, he thought it best to remove the busby before reading out the note.

'*Ragazzi,*' began George – without the hat.

Sensing something was afoot, Paula lifted her head up once more and locked her tear-filled eyes on George as he continued reading.

'*When you read this, I'll be on my way to my next adventure. Sorry for leaving you in the lurch. But what a finale! The cash in the tin is for you all to share. A little bit extra than we agreed. The fact is, I sold the garage last month, so I'm a bit flush. Don't worry, Jack. You've still got a job there if you want it. And I'm leaving you the Morris (but that still doesn't mean you can drive it like a maniac!). As I said last night, Paula, you get my Rolex. Try not to lose it. And Georgie boy, you are now the proud owner of a camera and projector. I know you'll put it to good use. I've also paid the rent on this old ruin for the rest of the summer. Be quite nice when it warms up, I reckon. OK. I think that's everything. Look after yourselves. Hopefully, our paths will cross again in the future. In this life. Or the next.'*

With the words still hanging in the air, all three of them froze in shocked silence. One, two, three. Calm over. The storm began.

'He's left me his Morris!' cried Jack.

'And he's left me his camera! And projector,' added George. 'Fuck! They're brand new! And you were right,' he said, turning to Paula. 'He's left you his Rolex. I don't believe it. Someone pinch me so I know I'm not still asleep!'

In the feverish atmosphere of excitement that filled the room, it was all the encouragement Jack needed.

'Ouch!' screamed George, jumping up from his seat to escape Jack's nipping.

'OK, OK, I'm awake, stop it!'

'You asked me to…' howled Jack, chasing him in hot pursuit around the table until they ended up locked in each other's arms, jumping up and down. In fact, they were so consumed by their own joy, they failed to notice that far from being thrilled to be the proud owner of a Rolex watch, Paula was once again in floods of tears. George knew that she liked Jack's boss, but there had to be more to it than that. Almost simultaneously, the boys fell from their embrace and took up positions on either side of their friend.

'C'mon, Paula,' said Jack, gently rubbing her back again. 'It'll be alright, you'll see.'

'Yeah,' agreed George, to the back of Paula's bleached mop. 'We've got this place for the whole summer.'

'And now I've got wheels, we can come here all the time. Nothing needs to change,' added Jack.

Except for the occasional sniff, an uneasy calm fell on the room. The boys looked at each other across Paula's hunched back. Shrugging his shoulders, Jack mouthed something to George, which he read as 'swimming's trouble'.

'Swimming's trouble?' George whispered back, unable to fathom out what Jack meant. Paula, however, had less trouble cracking the code.

'I'm not on the fackin' blob, you stupid wankers. I'm fackin' pregnant!'

Penny well and truly dropped, Paula returned to her hunched position on the table and tears and sobs filled the room once more. Unsure what to do for the best, Jack continued to rub her shoulders while George offered up some soothing phrases. But a new thought was slowly forming in George's mind. Oh my God. *Was that the reason Mancini had bolted?* Why he'd paid for the tower? And why he'd left them all those gifts? Had she told him? And then there was the night before. Hadn't she slept in his motor? Was he the father? It was all too much. George decided it was time to approach the elephant that had crept into the room.

'So…' he began nervously, fearing another flood. 'Did you tell him?'

It was clear from her answer that Paula knew exactly what he was insinuating.

'Fack off. It ain't naffin' to do with him!' she growled, in her usual Cockney. 'It's fackin' mine.'

Chapter Twenty-Seven

Carry on screaming

Thursday 14th November 2019 – 10.30pm – Ollie's flat, Kemp Town

If the mention of so many *Carry On* movies had whetted Ollie's appetite for a good old-fashioned British farce, the commotion that followed George's reaction to seeing Josh, would not have disappointed. Finding herself on stage with a comatose pensioner, Izzy jumped to her feet, gestured for the house lights to be turned up, and suggested that perhaps it was best for everyone to leave. Reminding him of a scene from *Titanic*, Ollie half expected her to shout, 'women and children first'. Though given the subject matter of the films, there were very few of the former and none of the latter. Not that you would have thought so from the sniggering that accompanied the chaotic exit. At least George was spared that, Ollie thought to himself on hearing the hysterical fits of laughter coming from the foyer. Although he had to admit, it would have been hard not to see the funny side. Especially when the colleague who had so meticulously operated the lighting and audio-visual equipment became so discombobulated by the turn of events that she began flicking switches on the mixer desk with the same reckless abandon that a one-year-old finds their way around a toy keyboard. As a consequence, the room was alternatively plunged into total darkness and blindingly bright light. And as if this weren't confusing enough, to add to the mayhem, the *Master and Manservant* film began to roll once again. Only this time, not across the screen, but across the faces of the escaping mob; the projector having been knocked over in the disorderly exit. In fact, had Ollie not leapt to the aid of his neighbour, he might have been tempted to film the slapstick comedy to enjoy later. Not that his assistance had proved very effective. Wafting Izzy's notes in front of George's face revived the old man for a moment, but the sight of Ken appearing in the spotlight with a glass of water triggered a new twist that was even more alarming than the first.

'Oh my God! The baby. Paula's baby. It was Jack's!' screamed George, pointing at Ken with one hand and placing the other over his mouth.

'You're Jack and Paula's son!'

Falling back slightly on hearing George's accusation, it seemed to Ollie that it was now Ken who was most in need of some TLC. And as his complexion turned as white as his hair, the cause of the commotion gradually became clear.

The likeness to Jack that George had seen in Josh wasn't a trick of the light.

It was a trick of nature.

Josh was Jack's grandson.

And Jack was Ken's dad!

Fortunately, by the time the shock of what George was suggesting had sunk in, the sound of giggling from the foyer had disappeared with the crowd, and the only people left in the café area were Ollie, George, Drew and the Pitts.

'OK. I think we need to get you home,' said Izzy to George.

'Good plan. You better all come back to mine,' added Ollie, knowing full well that this particular cat was not going to be put back in its bag tonight. George had some explaining to do, and half an hour later they were all crowded into Ollie's lounge, clutching hastily made G&Ts. Ken was the first to break the ice.

'But I thought Jack was gay!' he said, looking at George, who, seated in Ollie's only armchair, seemed to have regained his usual composure; if not his usual colour.

'Yes, I'd say that was his preference.'

'Looked pretty real to me,' said Josh, smirking.

'Oh. It was, dear!' said George, looking at the young man who not long before had caused him to keel over in horror. 'But I knew he swung both ways. We didn't really have a label for it like you do these days. But there was a lot of it about. And Jack was such a dreadful flirt. Boys and girls alike.'

'I suppose at that age most lads will shag anything,' said Ken.

'Charming!' said George theatrically.

'Sorry, I didn't mean you and… and… Mum,' said Ken.

Oh fuck! thought Ollie to himself. With all the excitement of the previous hour, he'd forgotten that the turn of events not only meant that Jack was Ken's dad, but also that the woman Ken had always thought of as his aunt, had actually given birth to him. News just in that he had been adopted by Paula's sister must have been devastating for Ken.

'Oh, don't worry, dear, I know what you meant. Like a dog with two tails,' said George, taking a swig from his tumbler. 'But as I said earlier, the two of them were very close. Thick as thieves I used to call 'em.'

From the way George was speaking, it was clear to Ollie that he wasn't the only one who had been moved by Ken referring to Paula as his mum.

'But she never once let on that Jack was your father,' continued George. 'Said it was a stranger; that she could barely remember what the fella looked like even – never mind his name.'

'But Jack must have suspected, surely? About the baby, I mean,' said Josh, bluntly.

'Well, yes. That had crossed *my* mind too. Especially after she told us that she was pregnant. I mean, he must have done the maths! But Paula was so determined the baby was her business and no one else's, even Jack might have questioned whether it was his. In fact, at the time, there was more reason to suspect Mancini – rather than Jack.

'Jack's boss!' said Ollie. 'Why?'

'Well, for a start, he left the morning after Paula told him she was pregnant. I remember her being beside herself when we discovered he'd gone. And then there was the note he left us saying that he'd paid the rent on the old tower for the rest of the summer. And if that wasn't enough, there were the gifts he'd left each of us.'

'Gifts!' Ollie repeated, perhaps a little too excitedly for the situation. *Could this plot get any thicker? Just wait until I tell Cameron.*

'Yes,' continued George. 'He left Jack his Morris. He was absolutely cock-a-hoop. Thought all his Christmases had come at once. But I just thought…'

'It was so you could look after the baby in the tower and still go to work in town,' interrupted Ken.

'Yes! Even the camera and projector he gave me. I thought that might have been to do with the baby, too.

Bringing up a kid ain't cheap. And as I said, the movies were quite a nice little earner.'

'Yes, I can see why you might have thought he was the father,' agreed Ken.

'At the time, yes. I thought Jack did, as well. But after tonight, I'm not so sure. In fact, maybe that's why he was so keen to play happy families at the old abbey. Perhaps he suspected all along that the baby was his.'

'Happy families?' said Ken.

'Yes. We pretty much spent every weekend at Coleshill after Mancini left. And once the baby started showing, Paula packed in her job at the theatre and moved in there permanently. Jack loved it. He even befriended a young nurse who was training to be a midwife at the Royal Sussex – to help us deliver the baby and that sort of thing. He was determined the baby would be safe,' said George, in Ken's direction.

But as reassuring as this may have been for Ken, Ollie's thoughts turned to the young nurse that George had just mentioned. Didn't Stephen say that the old dear they'd disturbed at St. Mary's on the night of Izzy's Hallowe'en party had been a midwife at the Royal? She'd be about the right age. And then suddenly it struck him. The aftershave he'd smelt in the cellar that evening. He knew it was familiar; it was the same scent that wafted out of George's handkerchief on the night he'd returned the letter. And the spectacles sniffed out by Mr Ben. They probably belonged to George, too. It certainly explained why he'd been wearing sunglasses during his interview with Izzy. *I wonder what they were doing in the cellar that evening.* Then, once again, the answer came to him in a flash. *Oh my God!* The photograph mentioned in the letter. I bet that was it. *I wonder if they found it.* What a dark horse his neighbour was turning out to be. It certainly was intriguing. But fearful he was missing out on the drama unfolding in front of him, he tuned back in just as Josh asked the question that was no doubt on everyone's lips.

'But why did Paula keep it secret?'

'That's exactly what I've been asking myself for the last hour, dear. Perhaps she wanted to protect my feelings. Jack was my boyfriend, after all! Or maybe she was waiting until the baby was born. It wasn't long after that…' said George, his voice trailing off into thin air. An uneasy silence fell upon the room for a few seconds. Being late and rather cold outside, there was none of the usual hubbub from the street below and the quiet was almost deafening. Then, just as Ollie thought he could bear it no more, the familiar haha-haha sound of a nearby seagull broke the spell and George was back in the room.

'Perhaps if Jack hadn't died, she might have told him,' he said, turning to Ken. 'But once he'd gone. I don't suppose it mattered anymore. Even when I bumped into her – years later – she made no suggestion that Jack was your father. In fact, I remember her saying she'd decided never to tell you that she was your birth mum. Said that it was better for you to think of her as your aunt; especially as you'd become so close. Of course, I still felt bad about it all – convincing Paula to give you up – but since she seemed pretty happy with the way things had turned out, over the years, I thought about it less and less. Until that bloody letter turned up out of the blue.'

Once again, the old man's train of thought came to a juddering halt. But just as Ollie feared the silence was about to return, George took a deep breath and was off again.

'Just think, if it hadn't been for Gracie popping her clogs, it would still have been our little secret. Fading away in some musty old hymn book. Trust it to have fallen into the hands of someone who knew me,' said George, pointedly in Ollie's direction.

'Well, to be fair, you're pretty well known around these parts,' said Drew, coming to his boyfriend's defence.

'Yes, I don't suppose it would have taken a detective to track me down. Especially with the internet. But that wasn't enough for old Gracie! Oh no. First the letter. Then those old mags. And finally, those bloody films.' George paused for a moment and took a gulp of his gin and tonic before continuing.

'I was pretty rattled at first, as you know,' he said in Ollie's direction, before turning to Izzy. 'But when you got in touch and told me what was on the reel of film you'd found… that it was just some grainy old pornos… I thought, what the heck. Nothing to be ashamed of. And the way you talked about them in your letter, it made me and Jack sound like some sort of queer pioneers.'

'Absolutely!' said Izzy, raising her glass.

'Right on!' agreed Josh.

'Obviously, I was curious to see my old self again after all these years. And Jack, too. I didn't for a moment think that they'd link us back to Paula and the baby. But when I saw this one coming towards me,' he said, turning to Josh. 'Well, I realised immediately that you were related to Jack. And the whole horrible mess just came flooding back.'

'Horrible mess?' interjected Ken, from across the room.

'If only I'd known that Jack was your father. I'd never have talked Paula into giving you away,' said George, staring directly at Ken. 'The day her sister came, Paula was in bits. Screamed the place down. And then tried to destroy everything to do with you. Clothes. Toys. Photos. Set fire to the lot. Even the home movies we'd made over the summer.'

'Home movies?' said Ollie.

'Yes. That's what I thought was on the reel; us playing happy families at Coleshill that summer. We used to film something every weekend. You know, with the camera Mancini left me. Sunbathing on the top of the tower. Country walks and drunken picnics. That sort of thing. And all the time, Paula getting bigger and bigger. It was so much fun,' Throughout this trip down memory lane, George's face seemed to Ollie to be alive with happy thoughts. But it was to be short-lived. A whisker's breath later, his blue eyes suddenly filled with tears, and the change in his voice signalled a darker mood entirely.

'But after Jack's death and helping to arrange your adoption,' he said, looking at Ken. 'I felt so ashamed about the whole thing. In fact, I remember at the time being quite relieved that the films and photos we took that summer had all gone up in smoke. That's why I was so distraught when the boys told me about a reel of film that had turned up in your attic. I didn't give a stuff about the pornos. What I thought was on the reel were those home movies we'd made when Paula was pregnant. And the possibility of it all coming back to haunt me after all these years. Well, it absolutely terrified me. I mean, what if people started asking questions? I just thought, I can't go through all that again.'

Obviously moved by the old man's distress, Ken put down his glass and knelt on the floor in front of George. But the old man was inconsolable.

'I'm so sorry, dear,' he sobbed. 'But Jack was dead. Mancini had gone. There was no way Paula and I could have looked after the child. Not in those days. We thought it was for the best. I'm so sorry.'

'Don't be silly,' said Ken, reaching for George's hand. 'I'm sure you did what you thought was best for everyone.

I don't blame you. And certainly not... certainly not... Mum!' he added, his voice cracking as the last word left his lips.

Thankfully, Ken's kind words did seem to provide some consolation for George, and by the time he had wiped away the tears with his handkerchief, he appeared to Ollie to have returned to his brighter self.

'If only I hadn't seen Jack's face staring down at me like that,' continued George, looking at Josh. 'Darker skin, but same eyes and freckles. Even the same sticky-out ears.'

'Steady on, old man,' laughed Josh.

'Sorry, but you do. Both of you, in fact,' he said, turning once again to Ken.

Reminded of Ken's recent Nosferatu get-up, Ollie had to agree with George; Ken's ears did stick out a little.

'If only I hadn't seen your face. I would never have had a funny turn. And you would be none the wiser.'

'None the wiser and worse off for it. I'm glad we know the truth,' said Ken.

'Yeah, me too. I love the fact my grandparents were so *sexually fluid*,' laughed Josh, polishing off his G&T and slamming it down on the coffee table. But before anyone could baulk at his comment, he turned the focus back onto George.

'So, what about Granny? What did she get?'

A look of confusion spread across George's face. Perhaps it took him a few seconds to realise Josh was referring to Paula and the gifts that Mancini had left them all.

'Oh, Paula you mean!' he said at last. 'She did best of all. Ended up with his Rolex! Worth a small fortune, I shouldn't wonder. No doubt she sold it, knowing Paula. Can't say I'd blame her if she did.'

'Oh my goodness!' cried Izzy.

'I know! Lucky cow!' agreed George.

'No, that's not what I meant,' she added, picking up the gift-wrapped parcel that Josh had been unable to hand over at the museum.

'The Rolex. We found it at the bottom of the trunk,' she said, handing it to George.

'Bloody hell. Didn't sell it after all!' laughed George, taking the package from Izzy and undoing the ribbon.

'To be honest, we thought it was fake! Another prop,' said Ken.

'Ooh, I shouldn't think so. I couldn't be certain, but I'd be surprised if it was. You should get it checked out. Anyway, I can't possibly accept it now you know how it came to be in Paula's possession.'

'Mmmm, that's the funny thing…' began Ken. 'There's an inscription on the back that looks like she intended to give it to someone on their birthday.'

Lifting the watch out of the box and turning it over, George squinted at the engraving.

'Sorry, dear,' he said to Ollie. 'Could you read it for me?'

Ollie took the watch off George and held it under the ceiling light.

'Happy Birthday Daddy – 10.08.65.'

No sooner had the words left Ollie's lips than the relative calm that had descended on the room turned to chaos once again.

'Oh God!' cried George, lifting one hand to his mouth in shock.

'What? What is it?' asked Ollie.

'The tenth of August. Jack's birthday. And the date of the crash! She must have finally told him the truth. On his birthday. That's why Jack was driving so fast that day. He was on his way back to me!'

Chapter Twenty-Eight

That Sun King feeling

Despite the sharp exit from the museum, Cameron's eagerness to get home was not so he could be away to his bed. Quite the opposite, in fact. He had work to do and he was keen to be reunited with his laptop. With that in mind, as soon as the cab they'd shared with Adam reached St. Mary's, he was out of the car and halfway down the street before Alex and Adam had settled the fare.

'What's the emergency, darling?' he heard Alex shout down to him from the hallway a few minutes later. 'Colostomy bag full again, love?'

'Sorry, hen?' he shouted back, already immersed in a slide presentation he was working on at the dining-room table downstairs.

'You. Jumping out of the car like that. Never even said goodbye to Adam,' continued Alex, finally in the same room.

'Seriously, doll! Do you think he even noticed we were there? On Grindr as soon as we got in the cab.'

'Yeah. Lucky bastard. I wish I was single.'

Being used to Alex's protestations about the supposed joys of bachelorhood, Cameron happily ignored his husband, lavishing his attention on his computer instead.

'Oh yes, Mr Bashir, there were three of us in that marriage,' Alex continued in his best Princess Di impersonation. Greeted with a disinterested 'ha ha' – Alex decided to try a different tack to get his husband's attention.

'So, who were you texting in the museum?'

'No one. I was filming,' replied Cameron, head behind his screen.

'Noooo! You do know piracy will be the death of cinema!'

'Aaaaargh! Jim laaaaad!' replied Cameron.

'OK. The films were hot. I'll give you that. But surely, you've heard of that thing… what's it called? Oh yes. The internet!'

'Aye, doll. But I didn't need it for the old wank-bank. I needed it for our gin campaign,' replied Cameron, lifting his head and smiling at his husband.

'Ooh gin!' said Alex. 'Good idea. Want one?'

'No ta. I need a clear head for my meeting tomorrow.'

'Just me then,' replied Alex, picking up his earlier theme of marital discontent. 'Drinking alone again. Poor wee wifey. It'll be the ruin of her,' he said mockingly, in Cameron's Scots brogue.

'Well, they do say misery loves company.'

'Aye, especially if it's served with ice and lime.'

This last quip caused Cameron to chortle and finally give his husband the undivided attention for which he had been fishing.

'It just came to me tonight,' said Cameron, looking up from his laptop.

'What did?'

'The perfect brand ambassador for Rakewell's Gin.'

'Who?'

'Bette, of course. And George.'

'Really?'

'Aye. Remember the line I told you about? *The gin that made the 60s swing!*'

'More like, *the gin that makes sixty-year-olds swing!*' scoffed Alex.

'Well, anyway. The client loved the line, just not any of the people we'd suggested to front it. Remember. Too expensive or…'

'Too straight.'

'Well, they don't come much camper than our Bette!'

'Or cheaper, I expect!' said Alex bitchily.

'Ha. If only they'd wanted *middle-aged and catty*. I could have put you forward.'

'Miaow!' purred Alex, clawing the air.

'But seriously, doll. They said they wanted someone with a bit of an edge. Just think how we could use Bette in social media. And the pornos. You're not telling me you weren't a little bit aroused by young George Gibbons!'

'They should have handed out cushions at the door!'

'Too right!' agreed Cameron, remembering the crossing and uncrossing of everyone's legs.

'And tissues! Though I think I preferred the other one myself,' interrupted Alex. Not that it really counted as an interruption since Cameron was on a mission and continued unperturbed.

'God, if we could get the rights to the films. I mean. Fuck. This is 360-degree marketing gold.' Seeing Alex was losing interest with this detour into ad-speak, Cameron closed his laptop.

'Oh, go on then. Mix us a G&T.'

'Rakewell's?'

'Hell, no! I'm helping 'em sell the stuff, I don't need to drink the pish too!' he said, slipping his computer into his briefcase. As he did so, his fingers brushed against the envelope containing the invite to the upcoming Winter Tableaux Vivants. With everything else that had been going on, he'd almost forgotten about it. Surprising really considering the commotion it had caused when they returned home after the wake at the Queens Arms. No longer, it seemed, was the opening of an envelope the punchline to a joke about someone for whom no event was too insignificant to attend. The fact was that in an age where postcards, birthday cards and party invites had been replaced by Facebook messages and texts, an item of post was, once again, a cause for excitement. Indeed, had he and Alex owned a tortoise-shell and brass letter-opener, it would have been the perfect occasion to bring it forth. Sadly, they didn't. So, the envelope that Cameron retrieved from his briefcase was rather more dog-eared than the sender of the beautifully crafted invitation would probably have wished.

'Must have taken Meena ages,' said Cameron, referring to the gold calligraphed address on the envelope, which he promptly threw into the hearth after removing the invitation.

He remembered that they had to go as Louis XIV's brother, Philippe le Duc d'Orléans and his lover, Philippe le Chevalier de Lorraine – but as yet they still had to decide who would be who.

'Hey, dawl. Have you thought any more about which Philippe you want to be for Maria and Meena's housewarming?' he said, as Alex was squeezing the juice of a lime into a large tumbler of ice.

'The Tableaux Vivants. I'm not sure.'

'Oh, come on. You're definitely the blond one in this relationship,' cackled Cameron, referring to the blond wig worn by the Chevalier.

'Fuck you!' said Alex, passing Cameron a fizzing glass of G&T.

'And I'm definitely Louis XIV's brother.'

'How so?'

'Well. I'm a top for one thing!'

'You're a top wanker, that's for sure,' replied Alex affectionately. 'Though I do rock a blond wig. Remember my Dolly?'

'I rest my case,' concluded Cameron, knocking back a large gulp of his cocktail. 'But what about costumes?' With that, Cameron retrieved his laptop and began searching for pictures of the couple from the recent hit TV series, *Versailles*.

'Voila!' he announced, spinning the screen around so Alex could see the image he'd blown up. 'What do you think?'

In the publicity photo, Philippe le Duc d'Orléans was wearing a long grey brocade jacket with matching waistcoat and slacks, while his lover, Philippe le Chevalier, was sporting a similar outfit in blue velvet and carrying a cane. Crowned with his beautifully curly blond locks, he was clearly the more ostentatious of the two men, and Alex squealed with approval.

'Good. Shouldn't be too difficult to find a couple of Versailles outfits. I'll swing by the party shop tomorrow. Get our order in before Christmas fancy-dress season kicks off.'

'Fantabulous, darling. But in what position shall we be *vivanted*?'

'Good question,' said Cameron, returning once more to his computer for assistance.

'Well?' asked Alex, getting a little impatient.

'Mmmm, just a lot of posing and snogging.'

'I seem to recall they did a lot more than that in the show!'

'Och well, how's aboot when they pull back the curtains, they find you on your back – legs akimbo – and me on top with my plus-fours round m'wee ankles?'

'With your cute little bot-bot smiling down at 'em all. Be worth it just to see the look on Izzy's face!' giggled Alex. 'Let's do it.'

Warmed by his husband's endearing smile and laughter, Cameron was not only considering the scene but just thinking about it re-awakened the spark of arousal that he'd felt during the film show. Their eyes locked over their drinks. It was clear Alex had had the same idea.

'Errrrm. Shall we…' he suggested.

'Fuck, aye!' replied Cameron, grabbing Alex by the hand and whisking him upstairs for an undress rehearsal.

Chapter Twenty-Nine

The native returns

Sunday 17th November 2019 – around midday –
An oak tree somewhere in between
Brighton and Rottingdean

True to form, the reason behind George's fainting fit had spread like wildfire in the days after the gathering at Ollie's flat. And with both Ollie and Izzy fanning the flames, it wasn't long before the news had reached the outskirts of Rottingdean.

'Por supuesto... of course... the old man at the farm and the baby things in the log-shed. It all makes sense now,' enthused Maria, getting the low-down from her sister. 'And why Paula made Ken feel so welcome in Brighton.'

'Yes, I know. Anyway, cariña, we're about to set off to the spot where Jack crashed his Morris. I'll text you when we're done. It's only a few minutes from your place.'

Squeezing herself into the back seat of their car a few seconds later, Izzy couldn't help but feel a little smug about the turn of events. Of course, it had been a shock at first, especially for Ken. But as he had said to her. *It's difficult to get really upset about people you've never actually met.* And since his adoptive parents had passed away a few years back, there wasn't even that to deal with. Not that he had ever seemed particularly close to them anyway. It was

George he felt sorry for. The relief on the old man's face, when Ken had reassured him that he'd made the right decision to give up the baby, spoke volumes. It had been a long time coming, but with everything out in the open, George was finally free. And more importantly for Izzy; so was she. Free to make the documentary she'd dreamed about ever since setting eyes on the films. All she needed to do was secure some funding and she could get started. And from what she'd read in an email that Cameron had sent her earlier, even that was looking quite promising. The message had been quite sketchy, but it seemed that a drinks client at his agency was interested in using George and the films in an ad campaign. A project that could be beneficial for both of them. *What did he mean, I wonder!* In fact, she was so busy thinking about what Cameron might be proposing, that before she knew it, they had arrived at their destination.

'Just there I think,' said George, from the front seat, pointing to a large tree a few yards ahead.

'Righty ho,' replied Ken, slowing down and pulling up opposite. As he did so, Izzy noticed a seagull amongst the leafless branches of the old oak upon which George's gaze was now focused. *Paula's wandering spirit again?* She dismissed the thought and undid her seatbelt.

'Are you sure you're OK with this, George?' asked Ken.

'Yes, dear. It's time,' he replied, opening the passenger door. Helped along by Izzy and Josh, seconds later all four of them were just a few feet away from the spot where Jack had breathed his last breath. Once at the tree, Ken swapped places with Josh and stood on the other side of George. From the corner of her eye, Izzy noticed Ken put his arm around the old man's shoulder.

'And this is definitely the place?' asked Josh, taking a photo of the tree on his phone.

'Yes, dear. I'm pretty sure it is. Of course, by the time I could bring myself to come, the Morris had been towed, and all that was left were a few bits of glass and a couple of broken branches. But that big old oak. I'd recognise it anywhere. This is where we...' Hearing the crack in George's voice, Izzy got a tissue from her handbag and passed it to him. As she did so, she noticed Ken tightening his grip on George's shoulder.

'I went to the service, of course. But it was a family affair. None of them knew about me and Jack, so I just sat at the back of the church. I watched them carry him to the hearse. But I didn't go to the crem afterwards. So, this is where we said our goodbyes,' he said, turning to Ken. 'Me and Paula... and you.'

'Thank you. That's good to know,' said Ken, before removing his arm from George's shoulder and walking towards the tree with the wreath they'd brought with them.

'Rest in peace, Dad,' said Ken, placing the garland of flowers at the foot of the tree.

'Yeah, rest in peace, Gramps!' added Josh, taking a photo of the wreath.

'We'll give you some time alone,' said Izzy, giving Josh one of her withering looks as she released her arm from George's. With that, all three of them walked slowly back to the roadside. Before opening the car door, Izzy looked back at George. In the few moments it had taken them to reach the car, he had walked towards the tree and was at that moment placing something next to the wreath. She was too far away to be certain, but from where she was standing it looked like a small blue tin. *Que curioso!* thought Izzy, as the seagull from before took flight and disappeared overhead.

Chapter Thirty

Oldest swinger in town

Sunday 24th November 2019 – 1pm – Old Music Library, Brighton

Housed in the town's former music library, Cameron's choice of restaurant for his meeting with George was no accident. He'd heard from Ollie about George's collection of old vinyl records and guessed the old man would be familiar with the building in its former guise. Just the thing to get him in nostalgic mood and open to my proposition, he mused. Turning up a few minutes before the agreed time, Cameron secured a table in the window where he would be able to see his guests arrive. It also gave him just enough time to peruse the menu and order a bottle of wine, which he hoped would oil the wheels of conversation. No sooner had the waiter scuttled off to fetch the plonk, than he saw Ollie and George appear through the heavy velvet curtain that hung over the doors during the winter months.

'Ollie! Over here,' he shouted, rising from his chair.

'This is my friend Cameron. From the advertising agency,' said Ollie.

'Very pleased to meet you,' said George. 'I think I saw you with Ollie at Gracie's wake last month.'

'Oh yes. I'm a huge fan,' flattered Cameron, shaking George's hand.

Keen to make sure George's attention was drawn to his best features, before taking his seat, Cameron removed his jacket and ran his fingers through his thick lion mane.

'Thank you, dear. Always good to meet a fan,' replied George.

'Aye. And the other night at the museum. I swear I have nae laughed so much in ages. I knew you were funny, but Christ! I nearly wet myself.'

'Oh, thank you. That's sweet of you. You can come again!' said George.

'I just might,' cackled Cameron, touching George's hand with the menu. 'Shall we order? And then we can get down to business.'

'Yes, good idea,' agreed George. But rather than turning his attention to his menu, it seemed to Cameron that the old man was more interested in the interior of the building.

'Gosh. This has changed a bit since my day,' he said, eventually.

'Oh yes,' said Ollie picking up the theme. 'It used to be the old music library, didn't it? Do you remember it back then?'

'Of course, dear. Whiled away many a Saturday morning flicking through the LPs they used to have here. Dusty, Sandie, Cilla. I especially liked the Righteous Brothers. Such lovely harmonies. We had a record player at the abbey, so I'd get a new stash every weekend. I haven't thought about it in years,' said George, obviously lost in another age.

'Are you ready to order, gentlemen?'

Like a needle being scratched across one of the long players George was reminiscing about, the question from the waiter seemed to bring him back to the present. The building was definitely having the effect Cameron had hoped. So, after they'd ordered their food, he cut to the chase.

'The thing is, George. We have a proposition for you.'

'Well, it's a long time since I've been propositioned in a restaurant,' said George, pursing his lips. 'Or anywhere else for that matter!'

'Oh, George. You crack me up. You really do,' chuckled Cameron, beginning to wonder who between them was the biggest flirt. 'Which is why I think you'd be great for a campaign we're putting together for a client of ours.'

'Yes. Rakewell's Gin. Ollie has told me a little about it. To be honest, I was surprised it was still going?'

'Just about. It's a relaunch,' said Cameron. 'And well, we'd really love you to front it.'

'Yes. As something called a brand ambassador, wasn't it?' replied George, looking at Ollie for reassurance. Cameron had already briefed Ollie to explain a little about his proposition in order for the idea to percolate. And the fact George had agreed to lunch was a good sign that it was brewing nicely. Feeling he was on a roll, Cameron reached into his satchel and pulled out an A4 piece of polyboard on which was written *The gin that made the 60s swing!*

'This is the tag-line we want to use.'

'Ha. Well, it certainly helped, dear,' said George. 'The gin I mean.'

'Right,' agreed Cameron, grinning at the joke.

'And what exactly would I have to do as a...?' asked George, waving his hand around like a visiting royal.

'As a brand ambassador?'

'Yes, dear. That.'

'Well, it all depends on you, really. Of course, we want you to front the brand as Bette. Drag is so big right now, and we think with the right team and budget you could be huge.'

Whether or not George still had a taste for Rakewell's Gin, Cameron wasn't sure, but judging by his performance at the museum, he was certain George had a taste for being in the spotlight.

'But it's not only Bette we want. Your past as a porn star is just perfect for a brand that wants to make itself relevant again.'

'Yes, Ollie mentioned that too. But I don't own them. The films, I mean. They belong to Izzy and Ken.'

'To be honest, that's a bit of a grey area,' continued Cameron, adopting his serious face. 'Legally speaking. And from what I understand, the museum can only make Izzy's documentary if you give your permission. So, there's certainly wriggle room.'

This last comment amused George for some reason and he gave a little giggle. *Tipsy already!* What a cheap date he is, thought Cameron, before ploughing on with his pitch.

'And, of course, there's the matter of funding. What we're proposing would make everyone happy. Izzy gets to make her documentary. We get our brand ambassador. And you get a nice little nest egg. Not to mention a boost to your profile. All we need is for you to say yes.'

'Oh, I see,' said George. 'And the films? How will you use those?'

'Well, we have a few ideas on the table. Gone are the days when we just get a celebrity to say something witty in a TV ad. Even a celebrity as funny as you,' added Cameron, turning up the flattery dial. 'People see ads in so many different ways nowadays. On the internet and in social media…'

'You know, George,' interrupted Ollie. 'Those videos I showed you on my phone.'

'That's right. There's even talk of showing them at film festivals!'

'Gosh!' said George, nearly spilling his wine.

'And who knows after that!' added Cameron, reaching for a breadstick. 'Of course, there'd be posters and press ads, but what we're really excited about is you. Your personality; your story. If we fund Izzy's documentary, Rakewell's Gin would be named as the sponsor. For the premiere, the client wants to go all out. Fancy venue in Soho. Q&A with a celebrity interviewer. Be great if Bette could give us one or two songs – perhaps a few jokes thrown in for good measure. There's even money in the budget for frocks and wigs. As Ollie told you, the client wants to target the LGBTIQ+ community first – before we go after the youngsters.'

'Oh yes. Get the gays, and the kids will follow!' said George, in an American accent, mimicking Rakewell's CEO, Donald Hunter.

'Yes, precisely! So, the guest list will be queer-tastic. And, of course, there'll be an endless supply of free Rakewell's Gin at the bar.'

'Careful, dear. You know how our people can knock 'em back. Don't want to bankrupt the company!'

'Too right!' agreed Ollie.

Unperturbed by his audience's interruptions, Cameron continued with his pitch.

'And then there's the merchandise. Calendars. T-shirts. Greeting cards. You could be a gay Bettie Page.'

Once again, the meeting was temporarily interrupted by the waiter. This time with their mains.

'And all you want from me is my permission to use the films and talk a little about how we came to make them?'

'Yes. Pretty much.'

'That's all?'

'That's all. Just your face. A few gigs and interviews. And your permission to allow us to use the films.'

Thanks to Ollie, Cameron was fully aware of Ken's adoption and how guilty George had felt about his involvement in it. If he was going to seal the deal, he knew he had to reassure George that this part of the story need never be revealed.

'How you choose to tell the story is up to you. It would all be agreed in the contract,' he said, staring directly into George's blue eyes for a moment before breaking the spell and delivering his winning shot.

'Then just sit back and count your money!'

Aware that the mention of money was a little crass, Cameron turned his attention to his duck à l'orange while George digested what he'd just said.

'And what sort of money are we talking?' asked George, calmly. *A little too calmly, in fact,* thought Cameron.

'Well, obviously we'd need to work out the finer details. But I think we could be looking at about 30 to 40 thousand.'

Perhaps the only shock at this juncture was that the piece of asparagus that George had just forked into his mouth did not shoot out across the table onto Cameron's plate.

'Well, it's certainly worth thinking about,' said George.

'Of course,' agreed Cameron, beginning to suspect his lunch wasn't the only wily old bird at the table.

Chapter Thirty-One

Jack-out-the-box

Monday 25th November 2019 – 11am – Upper St. James's Street, Kemp Town

Bzzzzzzzzzz.

'Hello…?' said a woman's voice.

'It's Georgie,' said George, staring at the speaker grill on the entry box. 'Georgie Gibbons.'

Instead of an answer, the door clicked open and George went in.

The sheltered housing where Jane Blythe had lived for the last 15 years was a 1980s complex of flats on the edge of Kemp Town village. An area largely made up of junk shops and eccentric little pubs – where dogs were as welcome as people – it was a pleasant contrast to the hurly-burly and neon lights of the bars that dominated nearby St. James's Street. Like George, Jane had lived in Kemp Town all her life. But until the previous month, they had not had a proper conversation for over 50 years.

'Ah, Mr Gibbons. Please, come in,' said Miss Blythe, greeting him at the door to her flat. 'You can leave your shoes and coat in here if you like,' she added, gesturing to the coat hooks and doormat just inside the entrance hall. Assuming this was not a request, George slipped off his slip-ons and pushed them against the skirting board next to a pair of fur-lined boots.

'I've just put the kettle on. Can I get you a drink, Mr Gibbons? Tea? Coffee?'

'Oh, thank you. Tea please. And do call me Georgie,' replied George, removing his overcoat and hanging it up in the hall. Though instead of inviting him to use her Christian name, as he knew she would have called it, she led the way to the living room and disappeared somewhere he assumed was the kitchen beyond.

Slightly disorientated by being abandoned in a strange room, George quickly scanned the lounge for clues to how Jane had filled the last 50 years. On a shelf unit that ran along one wall, there were a collection of photographs in ornate frames. Children mainly. *Nieces and nephews perhaps?* He was fairly certain she had never married. *Or were they children she had helped to deliver?* No doubt all would be revealed shortly. But then, to his complete surprise, he noticed someone who needed no introduction: Grace Davidson. In the photograph, Grace – wearing her mayoral chains of office – was presenting Jane and a group of nurses with an oversized cheque. *Well, I never. We've got more in common than I thought.*

Detective work complete, George took a seat next to the one that, by the looks of the old lady detritus around it, was Jane's usual perch – and tried again to ingratiate himself.

'Thank you for the other night at St. Mary's. I was in quite a state, wasn't I?' he called in the direction where she had gone. Coinciding with the whistle of the kettle and the sound of cups and saucers, George assumed his question had been lost in the cacophony of steam and crockery until Jane returned to the sitting room with a tray of tea things; and his answer.

'Yes, you were, rather. But when you told me what it was about, I couldn't refuse, could I? Jack. Still working his magic. Even after all these years!' said Miss Blythe, placing the tray down on a small table nestled in between the two armchairs.

'Yes, he's certainly got a lot to answer for. In fact, that's partly why I wanted to see you again. I would have got in touch sooner, but after the funeral…'

'Of course,' said Jane, glancing, or so George thought, at the photo on the shelf.

'Yes. Grace Davidson. I see you knew her, too,' said George, happy to have found a way to bring in their mutual friend. 'I couldn't help but notice the photo.'

'Oh, not *know* exactly. But I met her a few times. She did do a lot for the hospital. Especially for…' she paused '…for the local community.'

George knew exactly what she meant – and smiled.

'She was such a lovely woman. I'm so pleased she wanted to have the service at St Mary's. I helped do the flowers for her funeral. Such an honour.'

'Oh, Miss Blythe. They were lovely. You really did her proud.'

'Milk? Sugar? Mr Gib… Georgie,' she said, pouring the tea.

'Both please, two sugars, thank you… Jane.'

Milk and sugar added – and sensing the use of his Christian name was a further sign of rekindled warmth between them – George readied himself to broach the subject that had led him to seek her out once more.

'So…'

'Oh yes. The note you posted. Something about Paula wasn't it? I heard she'd passed away a couple of years back. God rest her soul. Younger than me, I think—'

'Yes...' interrupted George, unable to hold it in any longer. 'Do you think we were right to do what we did?'

Rather than being shocked by his question, Miss Blythe appeared to be undergoing a kind of meditation. She sighed deeply and stirred the sugar into her tea. *Had she guessed this was why he wanted to see her?* Her calmness certainly suggested that she had already given the subject some thought.

'You mean the adoption?'

'Yes.'

Removing the serviette from a plate of biscuits and placing it to one side, she looked him straight in the eye.

'What choice did we have? An unmarried mother. Only a girl herself really. Though she thought she knew it all.'

'Didn't we all?'

'Oh, I don't know about that. Jack and Paula, yes. But you were different. More cautious…' she paused for a moment to sip her tea. 'Certainly, it would have paid Paula to be a little more careful. That Italian fella was almost twice her age. Silly girl.'

'It takes two to… well, you know.'

'Yes, well. He probably knew how to do that, too!' she said, swallowing another mouthful of tea.

'Though Paula never actually said that he was the father, did she?'

'True. But why did he just disappear like that. Leaving you lot to…'

'Carry the baby?'

'Exactly. Never even came back for Jack's funeral. What a cad!'

The mention of Jack gave George a pang in his heart and caused him to take a sharp intake of breath. But instead of knocking his confidence, it gave him the courage to pursue his cause. He stirred the sugar in his tea and cleared his throat.

'It was Jack!'

Jane froze; her willow-pattern teacup suspended in mid-air.

'The father of Paula's baby. It was Jack,' repeated George, breaking the spell and allowing her to return the teacup to its saucer.

'No! I don't…' replied Jane, pulling a face that expressed clear disbelief in what she had just heard.

'Well, I bet that put the cat amongst the pigeons, didn't it?' she said, raising the cup to her lips and taking a big gulp. 'I always thought Jack was… you know…'

'He was. Mostly. I only found out he was the father myself last week!'

'You mean… all these years… you never…?'

'Not a clue!' he confirmed, reaching into his inside pocket to retrieve the photograph they'd found in the old hymn book. He'd been in such a panic the night at the church. As soon as they'd located it, George had hurried off before he'd had time to properly show it to her. 'That's why I wanted to come and see you. To do the right thing. To clear Mancini's name… the Italian fella… Jack's boss.'

As he said this, he passed her the photograph of them all on the pier.

'And to clear our consciences too.'

'Oh, my giddy aunt!' exclaimed the old nurse, returning the cup to its saucer to get a closer look at the photo. 'Look how young they look!'

'I know. A million years ago.'

In the photograph, Jack and Paula had their heads sticking through oval-shaped holes in a large painted picture postcard. Jack was playing the beach hunk, muscles bursting out of a red and white striped swimsuit. And Paula's head belonged to a small child dressed in Victorian sailor garb. Befitting the saucy postcard humour, across the top of the board were the words: YOU GET THE BEST MUSSELS ON BRIGHTON BEACH. Jane screwed up her eyes to focus in on those faces from her past.

'Jack. Acting the fool as usual. Not a care in the world. And look at the way Paula is gawping at him.'

Once familiarised with the old faces in the picture, Jane instinctively turned it over to read the message scrawled on the reverse.

'*Tad squiffy on the pier. 6th November '64,*' she read out aloud.

'I'm pretty sure this was the day they… you know. Jack and Paula.'

'Oh…' said Jane, placing the photograph on the table between them and returning her attention to her tea.

'I'm just guessing, but the timing fits. She knew she was pregnant in February and she gave birth in July.'

'Yes, you don't need to be a midwife to work that out. But why are you so convinced that the baby was Jack's?'

George paused a moment to compose his thoughts.

'Because I've met him! The baby; Jack's son. Ken. Remember, that was what Paula called him?'

Jane Blythe set down the teacup in the hollow of the matching saucer and stared directly at her guest.

'No!'

'Yes. And I've met Ken's son too. Jack's grandson. In fact, it was meeting *him* that gave it away. Josh, his name is. He's about the same age as Jack was when he died. And he's the absolute spit of him. Well, almost. A bit darker. Half Spanish in fact. And not as skinny. But his eyes and his freckly cheeks are just like Jack's.'

'And his sticky-out ears?' laughed Jane.

'Yes, yes. Those too!'

'Both Ken and Josh. They both have Jack's ears!'

'Oh my goodness! But how did you...?'

Over the next few minutes, George relayed the events of that fateful evening at the museum and afterwards at Ollie's flat. Noting her discomfort earlier – at the mention of anything to do with Jack and sex – he simply referred to the porn films as home movies.

'Paula actually saw Ken quite a bit when he was growing up,' explained George, trying to furnish Jane with the missing pieces of the mental jigsaw that he suspected she was creating in her mind. A concept with which, judging by the boxes of puzzles lining her bookshelves, he assumed she was rather familiar. 'Even more so when he moved to London in his twenties.' But rather than lightening the mood, George's recollections seemed to be having the opposite effect and tears began rolling down her cheeks. Sensing that the puzzle pieces falling into place had triggered a new question in her head, George leaned forward in his armchair and handed her the serviette that she had removed from the biscuits.

'We did the right thing, Jane. We truly did. I'm absolutely certain about that now. And Ken agrees,' he said, guessing his fellow conspirator was reliving that fateful day all those years before.

'Oh, Georgie,' she replied, wiping away her tears with the paper towel. 'That day the sister and her husband came to collect the little mite. Hardly a day goes by when I don't think about Paula's screams.'

'God, yes! Took both of us to stop her from running after the car.'

'I've never been able to forgive myself for convincing her to give him up.'

'No, me neither,' replied George picking up his teacup and taking a swig of tea. 'But I think Paula knew in her heart that it was for the best.'

Jane looked up from the photograph, directly into George's eyes.

'Really?'

'In her own way, yes. I mean, she never actually said we'd done the right thing. But giving Ken to her sister – at least that kept him in the family. And on the rare occasions that I bumped into her, she would always have some proud moment to relate. A promotion at work. Getting married. *My 'andsome nephew, Kenny* she used to call him,' said George, mimicking the fake Cockney accent that Paula had kept up until the end. 'Never saw them together though. In fact, the first time I met him was the other night. He's in his fifties now, of course. I reckon she was worried that I might have made the connection if I'd met him when he was younger.'

'Yes, you're probably right. Especially considering what you and his father used to get up to!' she blurted out, putting her hand to her mouth as if she didn't quite believe the words that had just come out of it.

'Jane Blythe!' goaded George, bursting into fits of giggles. 'You're wicked!'

'You must be joking. Jack was the wicked one. Buying me all those gin and tonics and convincing me that we could keep Paula's pregnancy secret. Can you believe I actually thought he was interested in me when we first met?'

She paused a moment and smiled.

'Until I met you, of course. Then it was as plain as the nose on my face.'

'Yes, I was a bit more obvious than Jack, wasn't I? Even then!' laughed George. This was turning out to be much more fun than he'd expected. With each moment that passed, the old Jane seemed to be returning, and he felt a sudden closeness to her and the fondness she had for Jack.

'But don't be so sure he was playing you. After all, we know he went over to your side – occasionally!'

'Oh, stop it, Georgie! You're terrible!'

They both cackled like a couple of witches. But despite her protestations, it was clear to George that she appreciated the possibility that Jack had indeed fancied her all those years ago. Even if the compliment had come 50 years too late.

'Oh well, we'll never know now, will we?' she said, once the giggles had died down.

'No, I don't suppose we will.'

'In any case, by the time I realised you were a couple, it was too late. I was already caught up in the whole affair.'

'Oh, come on. We made a great team.'

'Until… Jack…'

Like a door being slammed shut by a sudden gust of wind on an otherwise still summer's day, Jane's mention of Jack caught George completely off-guard. He cringed and breathed in sharply to buffer the force of the memory returning to the surface.

'Yes, after that there was no way we could have stayed at Coleshill,' he sighed. 'With no one to taxi us to and from the old place, Paula would have had to come back to Brighton. Who knows what would have happened to baby Ken if the authorities had found out?'

'Yes, you're right. But let's not talk about it anymore. I think it's best we let sleeping dogs lie,' said Jane softly.

'Yes, mum's the word,' agreed George, putting his index finger to his lips. 'Though I'd hate for us to go back to being strangers. I mean, I'd like us to be friends again.'

'Yes, I'd like that too,' said Jane, finishing off the dregs of tea from her cup and returning it to its saucer. 'And who's the fella in the summer hat?' she added, picking up the photograph and pointing to Mancini, whose head was poking through the hole above the neck of the buxom bather in a polka-dot bikini.

'That's Jack's boss,' replied George. 'Of course, you never actually met him, did you?'

'No, I didn't. Looks familiar though,' mused Jane, reaching for her glasses to get a closer look. Suddenly George started to feel a little bit faint. He couldn't risk waking any of those sleeping dogs they had just agreed to let lie.

'Oh bugger!' he cried, accidentally on purpose knocking over his teacup. As George suspected, rescuing the plate of biscuits took priority over her trying to put a name to a face, and he quickly returned the photograph to his inside pocket.

EPILOGUE

Let the tableaux vivant!
Saturday 30th November 2019 – 8pm –
Coleshill Abbey, Rottingdean

Finally, after weeks of anticipation, the day of the Winter Tableaux Vivants had arrived. In the run-up to what was being billed as 'the social event of the year', anyone lucky enough to receive one of the black and gold envelopes we saw the postman deliver all those weeks ago, had been busy at work. Costumes had been ordered. Accessories made. And Tableaux Vivants rehearsed. As for the hostesses, they had worked wonders turning the old log-shed into a pop-up theatre, complete with backdrop and steps up and down from a wooden stage. And once Josh, Kwan and Adam had set up the buffet, all that was required were some guests, which, at precisely 8pm, is exactly what arrived. Guided in by the cat's eyes that were the tower's upstairs windows – and the floodlighting that Maria had installed weeks before – the 12-seater minibus ponderously made its way down the pot-holed track to what remained of the abbey.

'Oh my God! It's like the Pharos Lighthouse!' exclaimed Izzy, referring to one of the famed Seven Wonders of the World. *Ah yes. Never one to miss an opportunity to remind everyone of her academic prowess was Izzy.* Though it has to be said, she's no fool. At one point, I even think she began to suspect there was more to my haha-haha-ing than meets the ear. But Paula's wandering spirit, I am not. She, I'm happy to say, is resting in peace with Jack and dear Gracie. And Izzy was right about the abbey. The new occupants had scrubbed the old place up pretty well. Even Cameron, who had been quite catty about the monthly renovation updates, had to admit to being a tad envious of what the girls had achieved.

'We really have to get our roof-terrace sorted,' he muttered to Alex, as they made their way up the torch-lit path.

'What a dump!' joked Drew under his breath to Ollie and Stephen, following close behind. And last but not least out of the minibus were Izzy, Ken and George, who, as guests of honour, had been invited to stay at Coleshill overnight and were greeted warmly by Meena at the garden gate.

'Really pleased you could make it at such short notice, George. We've put you in the guest room at the top. And you two are in *our* room tonight,' said Meena to her sister-in-law. 'Just make yourself at home and come and join us when you're ready.'

In fact, by the time George had settled into his room, it was time for the main event.

'Ladies and gentlemen, please take your seats. The Winter Tableaux Vivants are about to begin,' announced Meena from the stage, before disappearing behind the curtains.

As requested, everyone took their places in the two half circles of chairs that had been arranged in front of the stage. Except for George, who was directed to a throne-like armchair positioned in the middle of the front row. Heavily decorated in dried flowers and ceramic angels, it was from here that he would judge the best tableau of the night. So, once George had made himself comfortable – and Josh and Kwan had taken up their positions at either side of the stage, ready to pull back the curtain at the designated cue – the evening's entertainment could get underway. Of course, with all eyes firmly on the stage, no one would have noticed a solitary seagull sheltering between a gap in the battlements on top of the abbey's tower – the perfect viewpoint for me to draw this Brightonian tale to a close.

Sensing that something was about to happen, the crowd quietened down until the only sound that could be heard was the wind in the trees and someone shuffling behind the drapes that were hung across the stage.

'Let the tableaux begin!' shouted Meena.

Finally, the waiting was over. And while the other guests took their turn in the spotlight, over the next hour, George was treated to a pantheon of characters under the broad theme of 'Historical Lovers Through the Ages'.

First up was Venus, rising from a scallop shell, ready to inspire the waiting Sappho to write her famous homage. This tableau caused a gasp from the audience as much for Meena's strategically placed merkin, as for the pose itself. Arranged chronologically, next up was Adam's interpretation of the moment Narcissus falls in love with his own reflection in a pond. Unable to find a 'plus one' willing to play his doppelgänger, Adam had only needed a red toga, a crown of leaves and a large rococo framed mirror – borrowed from his café-deli – to recreate the legendary egoist. Simple and effective, it was no doubt also annoying for those who had spent a good deal more time and money on their own costumes. That is to say; almost everyone.

The exceptions to this, perhaps, were Ken and Izzy, who had once again managed to kit themselves out from Paula's hoard. Immediately recognisable to all from *The Rides of March,* was Ken's Marc Antony costume. And Izzy's Cleopatra outfit looked suspiciously like the wedding dress she'd worn as the scary heiress for her Hallowe'en party; dyed black and without the padding, but with feathers and beads from the Native American outfit worn by Jack in *Wild, Wild West.* Moving away from the ancients, Stephen and Mr Ben brought the audience the medieval magic of Guinevere and Sir Lancelot in a scene where the tragic queen – played by Stephen, of course – is saved from being burned at the stake by her knight in shining armour; Mr Ben, wrapped from head to tail in tin foil. Looked forward to by everyone as much for the expected urinary mishap from Mr Ben as for Stephen's interpretation of the mythical lovers, as it turned out, the only ones in danger of wetting themselves were the audience – such was the absurdity of the tableau. Disappointing as this may have been for anyone looking forward to seeing Sir Lancelot cocking his leg against the tragic queen, Cameron and Alex's decision to depict a scene of bedroom rumpy-pumpy for their tableau of the two Philippes, did go some way to make up for the lack of impromptu leg-shagging which often accompanied the aforementioned hound's bladder blunders.

And finally. To round off the evening's entertainment, the audience was transported to the infamous Albemarle Club in 1896, where Drew, dressed in straw boater and cricket whites, made a dashing Bosie. And Ollie, dressed in a green-padded smoking jacket and velvet fez, an equally impressive Oscar Wilde.

'Bravo, bravo!' shouted George, as Ollie and Drew climbed down from the stage to join the others for an orgy of backslapping and mutual appreciation. Though for most, the excitement was owed more to the relief that this part of the evening was over.

But was it over? An announcement from the stage suggested otherwise.

'Ladies and gentlemen. Please remain seated,' announced Venus, standing next to one of the curtain pulleys to the side of the stage.

'In honour of our very special guest, we have one final tableau of the evening,' continued Sappho, picking up the theme.

Surely everyone had done their turn, hadn't they? But wait. Where were Josh and Kwan? And why were Venus and Sappho standing in their places?

'Ladies and gentlemen... please put your hands together for...' announced the girls in unison as the swish of the curtains drowned out the name of the final tableau vivant. It was, however, of no consequence since no one was in any doubt whom it depicted.

Dressed in a red silk dressing gown and boxer shorts, Josh was immediately recognisable as his grandfather in the opening scene of *Boxing Clever*. And with a blond wig fashioned into a crew cut, Kwan made a passable George from the same film. Though not quite up there with the previous rollcall of historical lovers, few in the audience would question Jack and George's legendary status as romantic leads in the mythology of this wonderful city by the sea. The crowd gasped. Josh threw a wink at his grandfather's ex-lover. And at some point, between the laughter and applause, George thought he heard the sound of a seagull somewhere nearby. You see, there is one more twist to the tale. One more secret that must be revealed, before I fly away and leave these Brightonians to their fun.

'Oh bugger, I almost forgot!' said George under his breath, as the cheers and clapping died down around him. As I had hoped, my haha-haha from the top of the tower jogged George's memory about his gift for the Pitts. So, after congratulating Josh and Kwan for the final tableau, he asked them all to join him in his room.

'Oh, George! You star!' said Ken, looking at the face of his father staring back at him from the framed photograph of Jack, Paula and Mancini on the pier.

'Well, it was either that or the one from *Adonis Body!* And I'd like to hang on to that one, thank you very much!' George laughed. 'Of course, this one's got your mum in it too.'

'But where did you... I mean... didn't you say that all the photos had been lost in the fire?' asked Josh.

'I thought they had. Until that letter turned up with the mention of a photograph. I didn't think much of it at first. But when I remembered what it was of – and that I'd used it to mark one of the hymns sung at Churchill's funeral service – I went back to St. Mary's to look for it. And there it was. Right where I'd left it. Shoved in between the pages of 'Mine Eyes Have Seen the Glory of the Coming of the Lord'.'

'Ha, well, they have now!' laughed Kwan, who'd tagged along with Josh.

'*Oh you!* I can see I've got competition!' laughed George.

'And who's the chubby lass in the swimming costume?' asked Josh.

'That's Jack's boss, Michael. Well, Michelangelo actually. Italian...' began George, before abruptly changing the subject. 'Anyway, I'm so pleased you like it. Right. I don't know about you lot, but I could definitely do with a top-up after all those tableaux. Shall we re-join the others before they run out?'

'Good idea!' said Ken. 'And we can take these daft outfits off too!'

'Speak for yourself, darling,' said Izzy, stroking the snake arm-bangle that she was wearing for her role as Cleopatra. 'I've never felt more... queenly!'

And with that, Ken, George and Izzy, made their way down the stairs to the others. Josh was about to follow when...

'Hang on a minute, Josh,' said Kwan.

'What? I'm gagging for a piss!'

'I think you'll want to see this.'

'Not now, Tiger!'

'No. *This!*'

Turning back into the bedroom, Josh was relieved that the 'this' to which Kwan was referring, was, in fact, one of the flyers that they had handed out to advertise the candlelit vigil they'd organised for Grace on the day she died. Though a little creased, the photo of Grace had survived well, considering it had been in Kwan's pocket since the day of the vigil. They both re-familiarised themselves with the image, which judging from the permed hair and large glasses, probably dated from the 80s.

'Look!' said Kwan, holding the flyer next to the framed photo that George had just given to Ken. 'The Italian bloke. Jack's boss.'

Josh looked at one photo.

And then at the other.

And then back to the first.

'No, it can't be!'

'It is. It totally is!'

'OMG. You're right. It's Grace!'

THE END
(for now)